Sanguine Dawn

Ankeshwar Mishra

Leadstart
INKSTATE

ISBN: 978-93-90040-51-3

First published in India 2021 by Leadstart Inkstate
A Division of One Point Six Technologies Pvt Ltd

Sales Office:
Unit No.25/26, Building No.A/1,
Near Wadala RTO,
Wadala (East), Mumbai – 400037 India
Phone: +91 969933000
Email: info@leadstartcorp.com
www.leadstartcorp.com

Disclaimer: The views expressed in this book are those of the Author and do not pertain to be held by the Publisher.

Editor: Vaibhav Pathare
Cover: Ami Parekh
Layouts: Victor Patali

*This book is dedicated to my mother Mahasunder Devi and
father Late Dharni Kant Mishra.*

About the Author

The author has a broad knowledge of the history of India and the present socio-economic condition of the country. The author has done his MA in Economics and an MBA in Finance. The author is a government employee. He is working as a Deputy Director of Administration in a reputed national institute under Ministry of New and Renewable Energy. The author has served in various departments of the Government of India like the Ministry of Defence, various scientific and research organisations under Ministry of Science and Technology. The author has a deep passion for reading and writing and with this book he wants to connect, communicate & create awareness among people all over the globe.

One

It is a moonlit night, the stars are shimmering, the scent of jasmine is prevalent in every nook and corner but the atmosphere is filled with an unusual silence, calm, stillness and resentment. Three days back the terrorists had attacked the army camp. The attack had left 21 soldiers martyred.

Such cruel incidents on national or international scale totally shake mankind in general. Although in a few days after the incident, everything returns to normalcy after some wave of anger, pain, opposition, candle march, etc., except for those who are family or directly related to the martyred soldiers.

In this backdrop, three girls who are pursuing graduation, namely Dorothy Jones, Gurmeet Kaur, and Parul Patel arrive in a restaurant at 8 p.m. for dinner which was a pre-planned one.

After common formalities, the menu of the dinner is decided and the order is given to the waiter. Dinner will be served in almost half an hour. Their chatter continues.

Dorothy Jones: Hey, did you speak to Aakanksha? How is her father now?

Parul Patel: Yes, he is out of danger; he has been shot in the right shoulder. By the grace of God, he is safe now but 21 soldiers from his platoon were killed in that incident.

Gurmeet Kaur: Nowadays, everywhere in the world, not a single day passes without a terrorist act. Somewhere they attack army camps and sometimes common people are crushed by trucks in public places. Now the terrorists are not sparing even the pious religious places like Temples, Mosques, Churches, and Gurudwaras, etc. In fact, they have found novel ways to attack these religious places.

Parul: Right, just like the World Environment Day, World Health Day, World Yoga Day, etc. are celebrated, similarly, there is a queue of 11 September (the day of the terrorist attack on WTC in the USA), 13 December (the day of Indian Parliament attack), 26 November (Mumbai terror attack), etc. of terrorist attacks days.

Dorothy: All the countries of the world should take some solid steps in the leadership of the United Nations Organisation to eradicate terrorism from the root. Only then, the world can be freed from this monster named terrorism.

Gurmeet: Those countries who watched these terrorist activities happen in other countries as silent spectators and forget some action on it, they even shied away from giving any reactions on it, have gradually been affected by this heinous monster and are seeking a solution for it now.

Parul: If we see in a broader aspect, there are many problems in the world that are complementary to each other. Poverty, illiteracy, unemployment, law and order, electricity, water, infrastructure, corruption, drugs, smuggling, arms, no assurance of justice to poor and backward, etc. are some of them. Terrorism is also one of them. If the real cause behind all these problems is found and the problems are suitably solved, then, the problem of terrorism will also be solved along with it,

Dorothy: If we see thoroughly, the presence of nuclear weapons in the world is the biggest problem for me. Moreover, the problems of global warming, climate change, and environmental pollution are the most affecting ones. Actually, the problem of nuclear weapons is such a huge one and there is such a big number of these weapons present in the world that Earth can be destroyed a hundred times over. Even if these weapons fall in the hands of wrong people by mistake, what will happen to the earth and to the creatures inhabiting it? So, these nuclear weapons itself need to be destroyed which have a destructive capacity of destroying the earth and all its living creatures.

In the same way, the temperature of Earth is increasing day by day due to increase in greenhouse gases. The earth is getting hotter slowly, the snow on the mountains and poles is melting, small islands and coastal areas are on the verge of submerging in the ocean. Climate is changing very fast; the rains are irregular and monsoon is coming late every year. Environmental pollutants are not only contaminating water, land, and air but also becoming hazardous to life in many ways day by day. Each year millions of deaths occur due to environmental pollution.

Gurmeet: Yes, all the problems we discussed are very serious but they can be solved by a strong will.

Dorothy and Parul speak together: But how?

Gurmeet: "Well, today's children are the father of tomorrow, so if they are educated, made wise, cultured and awareness in created among them in a proper manner, then there will be no corrupt people and terrorists tomorrow. Illiteracy and poverty will be eliminated from society. Smuggling and drug abuse will automatically come to an end in society. The dreams of *"Sarvey Bhavantu Sukhinah"* (may all become happy) and *"Vashudhaiva Kutumbakam"* (the world is one family) will be realised instead of making arms and ammunitions.

A child who is taught universal brotherhood/cosmopolitanism from childhood, for whom will he/she make nuclear weapons or keep or use against? That child will help destroy the nuclear weapons like *"Bhasmasoor"* (one who burned everything) by himself or herself.

If we impart such knowledge and wisdom to our children that they take water, forest, and land as a means of co-existence and not a commodity, so that they keep it clean and emphasize on sustainable growth, the problems of global warming, climate change, and environmental pollution will not even appear.

A child who is brimming with love for nature, why shall he/she cut a tree or write the name of his/her lover on it, during youth? They will plant a sapling in their lover's name instead, and why trees only, they will plant a garden full of flowers and fruits in the name of their love. They will be more interested in eco-friendly transportation running on biofuel and not in costly and more polluting vehicles.

The children who are born and brought up in an excellent environment will never be vindictive and will be filled with a motto for the welfare of the world. Therefore, if we focus on the complete development of our children, all the problems in the world will be solved automatically. It will be like to do one thing well and all is done. In marketing terms, this is the combo pack solution for all the problems.

Let us see the example of Israel. Here, when a mother conceives, from that very moment she starts getting special attention. She is provided with a nice environment and motivational stories are read to her. After she gives birth to the child, special care is taken to ensure health, attitude, culture and behavioural training and teaching to the child. As a result, you can see how this small country is leading in every sphere of life and world. If such an atmosphere is created in the whole world, the Israelites may also destroy their arms and nuclear weapons."

Dorothy and Parul very much agree to Gurmeet and talk about their specific problems and give innovative ideas to solve them. Meanwhile , the waiter serves the dinner and they finish it. After some chit chat, they leave for their hostel.

In the hostel when they reach their rooms, they are very happy and chirpy. All three friends promise to one another that they will not work only on a single issue or for personal gains but will dedicatedly work for the welfare of society, nation and above all, the world.

Their chatter started on a sad terrorist incident and ended on a happier note of the happy future of children, a world free of nuclear weapons and environmental pollution. The best part of this event is that these girls who do not know their own future, think about and weave a better future of the universe.

Later on, they continue their studies and keep meeting, talking and arguing on various social, economic and political issues including "Khap Panchayats". The studies on which the social, human and worldly future of these three friends depends are not only academic and educational but also social, economic, environmental and political, etc.

There are some people who are lost in beautiful romantic imaginations for the future. They feel that the next moment will be theirs. A joyful message will come, life will change as their wishes, all their presumptions/speculations will be completed and all the dreams will come true. Meanwhile, the other power keeps working. Time flies fast. When one is busy, happily dreaming for the future, the present which is most important, passes quickly, and never comes back. We, humans, realise this when it is out of our reach and has already passed.

There are very few people who understand the value of this time in time and recognise it. This is what happens with these friends as they are concentrating more on the problems of the world rather than studies. During this period, they are unable to solve their own problems i.e., their courses have not been completed yet and examination dates arrive. It is also true that when someone thinks more about other problems, then God starts thinking about their problems. This is what happens with these three friends.

After the dates of examinations are declared, these three friends' study wholeheartedly. They appear in the exams and pass with very good marks in their respective subjects.

Meeting and separation are the laws of nature. Happiness- sorrow, day-night, sunrise-shade are inseparable parts of life. Those who are wise, never deviate during adversities of life and remain humble in good times without being proud and arrogant. These friends also display the level of knowledge acquired. They decided that after being together for so much time, now at the time of parting, we will not be emotional. They organise a grand farewell for themselves. So, at a time when most of the courageous and patient persons lose their calm and cool, the girls give a special farewell to themselves where the organizers and those who are getting separated are no different.

The trio promise without getting their eyes wet that whenever and wherever they need one another, they will stand in unison, help one another and work for the welfare of the universe. They also promise that they shall rise beyond the individual benefits and work for the society, nation, and mankind. Even dogs and cats live their lives and bring up their young ones. Since we are humans, we are rational and educated, so we have to think and act beyond ourselves and do something good for the whole world.

Two

Every day many new ideas, discussions, debates, and suggestions keep coming to life but there are some events or occurrences that leave their imprint forever in our hearts. Even if we wish, we are unable to stop until we reach that goal. All these three friends Dorothy Jones, Gurmeet Kaur, and Parul Patel had promised each other that they will work for the society, for the welfare of the world and humanity in general. They will work hard and will be unstoppable but in reality, they were lost in their personal lives. Between all this, there was one person who was restless, and that was Gurmeet Kaur.

If you want to do something really big, first of all, there should be proper planning. After that, it becomes easier to implement. But what to do? How to do? For whom to do? What to initiate? Gurmeet was perplexed by all these questions. There are many problems in society, which one should be tackled first? One that is more serious or the other that is urgently required to be solved for the sake of society? Gurmeet was in this state of confusion for a while. But where there is a will, there is a way.

Once you are more concerned about humanity than yourself, you are thinking for the welfare of the universe itself, you find the means and ways by yourself and God is unable to stop himself from helping such people.

It was a bright sunny afternoon; roads were full of vehicles running at their own speed and people wear busy with their daily routine.

Gurmeet was driving when she saw the scene which shook her from inside out. She saw some dogs and a child-eating leftover food together from the leaf plates lying beside the road near a house.

Gurmeet parks her car in the roadside and asks the whereabouts of that child. She gives some eatables from the car to that child. She also gives him some money and is back to her home now. She shares this incident with her mother and then and there decides to begin her social work for the welfare of children. Moreover, these children are the future of the nation. If they are made better, the future of society will be better.

To the parents, the happiness of their children is supreme. In general, all the parents in the world wish that their children have a good education that leads them to be a better human as the parents will also get a good name with the name and fame of their children. Some parents give freedom to their children to study and work as per the children's interests.

But most of the parents want their children to fulfil their dreams that they could not realise themselves. Either this dream could be of becoming a bureaucrat, political leader, businessman, industrialist, actor or philanthropist, etc. But Gurmeet's parents have given her full freedom to study and work according to her own interest and convenience. Gurmeet believes that one need not be a servant for social service or for the service of the nation. We can work better without being in service as we can be more independent to work as we wish. Her parents do not impose their will on her to accomplish their unfulfilled dreams and wishes but rather bestow her with the freedom to begin to work as a philanthropist. She can also use their property however she wants to use it.

Gurmeet starts her social work on a small scale. She helps in admitting small rag pickers and beggar children to the school. She arranges for uniforms, books, stationery, etc. for them. The problem does not end here. There are some parents who say that my child earns this much from begging every day, so if you pay me this amount, only then I will let the child go to the school, otherwise, we will send him/her for begging only.

Gurmeet is very sad to find how parents can think so badly for their children. If somebody sends them to school, they ask for money which is equal to their begging or daily wages. Whatever happens, Gurmeet starts working for her campaign tirelessly. Although in India, the right to education for the children aged between 6 years to 14 years is a constitutional right, it becomes very difficult for her to get it implemented. She has to take the help of many means to make parents understand or sometimes even for one parent to know the value of a better future for their children. Accordingly, she also has to threaten them sometimes.

It was beyond her imagination to understand that parents can be a hindrance to something which is meant for their child's bright future. It always happens that when a person comes out of the world of books, reality shatters those bookish theories. Anyways, Gurmeet is busy with her work without any greed and fear.

If you do social service or philanthropy through your own resources, then it will be a limited one. If you are as rich as Bill Gates or Warren Buffett then no issues, but for a normal middle-class person, it cannot run long on his/her own resources. Gurmeet also establishes an NGO and looks for funding resources. There are many people who come ahead to support her, by themselves. During all this, she comes in contact with a man named Munna.

Munna is a tall, large, fair and smart guy who introduces himself as a student of Delhi University. Gurmeet wants to know more about him but he does not talk much about himself. He tells only that he is not a believer in caste, religion, etc. Although he is an atheist, still he can go either to a temple or a mosque. When he is asked about his home and family, he says that all has been destroyed and has nobody in this world to call his own. When asked to which state he belongs, he says that basically he is from Jammu and Kashmir but now he has migrated from there. There is not a single survivor in his family. Gurmeet inquiries about the cause of this catastrophe and he informs her that it was due to the firing between the Indian Army and terrorists. But he does not know who is responsible for the devastation of his family.

Munna extends his wholehearted support to Gurmeet's philanthropic works. It seems as if Munna and Gurmeet complement each other and both are made for this pious social work only. Gradually they become good friends.

Meanwhile, to collect money for the NGO, Munna and Gurmeet visit several institutes and organisations. Some donate very easily and some of them pay after lengthy pursuance. At some places, they are asked even for a bribe in lieu of a donation to the NGO. Once they have to face such an awkward situation during their visit to an organisation for funding. Munna and Gurmeet are made to sit in the visitor's room. Munna has been called inside and Gurmeet has to wait outside. Munna is offered more funds than what has been demanded by them only if he sends Gurmeet to the officer concerned for one night. Munna comes back to hastily. Gurmeet asks if something has happened. Munna is angry and says we will never come here again. These people talk about rubbish. In spite of all these difficulties they go ahead with their never say no and selfless attitude.

Munna has rented a house in the vicinity of Gurmeet's house. Now they have started spending a lot of time together. Previously Gurmeet was praised by the society for her philanthropy but now whispers about her are going around. People have started raising finger on Gurmeet's character.

There was something else occurring in the life and mind of Munna. He did not want to marry Gurmeet and spoil her life. He wanted a relationship with Gurmeet without marriage and Gurmeet insisted on marriage. Munna was interested in using Gurmeet as a means to his goal. He needed a step at this juncture of his life so that he could implement his future plans by stepping upon it. Gurmeet could prove to be that desired step for him since all his physical needs seem to be fulfilled through her.

Gurmeet's neighbour and closest friend Geeta alerts her against Munna. She tells her that he is an outsider and you know nothing about his home, family, and character. It would be better if you keep a safe distance from him. First of all, you should investigate all the facts about him and then do what you want, either marry him or have a live-in relationship.

There comes a tender phase in an age when heart and hormones tend to affect your decision more in comparison to the brain and mind. You have to very carefully control this hormonal change resulting in the overall change in yourself by being rational and that too efficiently and patiently. Maximum people lose control over themselves during this period of change. Animal instinct prevails over reason. Human is unable to decide between good and bad. A small mistake during this phase proves big for the whole life. A courageous, patient and reticent girl like Gurmeet wins the heart of the society but loses her own heart and decides to marry Munna in a hurry.

A girl who wishes to marry someone should want to know all about him before that decision. Gurmeet is not an exception, but Munna speaks nothing about himself. He changes this topic cleverly giving it an emotional turn.

Love is believed to be blind, which is unable to differentiate between good and evil. In this case, it seems to be deaf as well. Gurmeet is repeatedly alerted by Geeta but she is not ready to see or listen to anything.

Gurmeet and Munna tie the wedding knot in a simple ceremony even without the approval of Gurmeet's parents. Gurmeet asks

Munna to leave his rental house and move into her home but Munna keeps that rented house and most of the time he lives in her home. As a routine, he regularly visits the rented house for a while.

Gurmeet is wholeheartedly absorbed in her work. The scope of her work increases with time. She had started with children's education and sending them to school and now it has stretched up to the settlement of elderly people. Meanwhile, Gurmeet misses that support from Munna which he provided her earlier.

Despite Gurmeet's marriage with Munna, Geeta has doubts regarding him. She could not accept him but after marriage, she has stopped discussing this topic with Gurmeet. Still, whenever she meets Gurmeet and talks to her, she alerts Gurmeet from Munna rather jokingly.

Munna's mobile number is flooded day by day with national as well as international calls. He gets maximum calls after midnight till 5:00 a.m. in the morning. During the period a radical change is visible in his nature, behaviour, food, ideas, etc. One cannot suppress one's true nature for long. In spite of hiding it for a while, gradually, the real face comes out. Now, Gurmeet also has doubts about Munna's work.

One day she is at Geeta's place. They have been in chatting for long.

Geeta: So tell me, is everything alright between both of you?

Gurmeet: "No dear, do not tell it to anyone as I am sharing this with only you. Earlier you had doubts about Munna and now even I doubt him. Most of his phone calls come after one or two a.m. at night. Whenever he attends those calls, he comes out for the bedroom and discusses a plan. I married him without the permission of my parents. Now it seems that I have been trapped in the wrong place. What shall I do now? I do not understand. Please advise me, what to do?"

Gurmeet said and her voice choked.

Geeta hands over a glass of water to Gurmeet and says in a light manner that first of all, you should drink a glass of water. This lightens the heaviness of the situation. Then Geeta speaks as to how she is unable to share much with Gurmeet. Yesterday she saw many people come to his rented room in a vehicle that looked very dangerous.

Gurmeet: I think he is planning something, may be hatching a conspiracy. I am afraid if something untoward happens. Tell me, what shall I do now? What can we do? I am totally confused and much worried.

Geeta: See, I have an idea. If you find it ok, then let me know it may solve all the problems possibly.

Gurmeet: What is that?

Geeta: Look, I have a friend Navjot here. Her husband has a shop of CCTV cameras and he does secret recording as well. You send Munna somewhere or whenever he goes out, you can plant CCTV camera and recorder in your home and his rented house. We will ask Navjyot to make her husband record both audio and video. Later, we can see and listen to them. This will certainly give us a clue about his mind-set and also about his plans.

Gurmeet: Yes dear! The idea is very nice but it is possible only if he goes out. Otherwise, it is a very sensitive matter and he may be careful if it leaks out. We will not be able to know anything and obviously, it may affect our relationship as well.

Geeta: Send him out without further delay now.

(Before Gurmeet could speak, Munna called her up and said that he has to leave for Mumbai for some urgent work. His flight is at 7:00 p.m. today and he will reach home within an hour she should pack her clothes and keep them ready).

Geeta: What happened?

Gurmeet: He is going to Mumbai today by the 7:00 p.m. flight.

Geeta: Very nice! Now, what do you think about CCTV and recording?

Gurmeet: Great idea. Please talk to Navjot as it is a very sensitive matter and should not get leaked out. Only one or two people should come and install the latest recording instrument at my place and Munna's rented space.

Geeta: Wait! I am calling her.

Gurmeet: You speak to her at your level and tell me later on. I am going to pack his clothes, etc.

Geeta Ok bye, take care.

Gurmeet is now at home and packs Munna's clothes, shaving kit, toothbrush, etc. Munna comes back and leaves for the Delhi Airport very soon. In the meantime, the latest camera and recorder are installed in both places. Only Gurmeet, Geeta, Navjyot, her husband and Gurmeet's mother know about it.

Munna stays in a hotel for four days after arriving in Mumbai. After executing his work, he moves to Varanasi. He spends four days in Varanasi as well. From there he advances towards Chandigarh. Once again, he suddenly plans for Ahmedabad and he leaves for Ahmedabad. Munna is in Ahmedabad and executing his work there. Meanwhile, Gurmeet calls him to inform him that her maternal grandmother is unwell and she will visit her at Amritsar with her parents. She also tells him that she will stay there for about one week.

Munna says that at present he is in Ahmedabad and his work is almost finished. Tomorrow he will be back in Faridabad. On his way to Faridabad, Munna is very happy to realise that Gurmeet will be in Amritsar for a week as the crucial moment of his life has approached very near now. In this situation, Gurmeet's presence could be harmful to him, whereas her absence could be a blessing in disguise as he could use her home and resources according to his needs and convenience. There will be no concern that somebody is watching everything, who can leak about his conspiracy. Two days after Gurmeet leaves for Amritsar, along with her family, Munna comes back home after his trips to Mumbai, Varanasi, Chandigarh, and Ahmedabad respectively. They could not meet each other. Both of them have one set of keys with themselves, so they have no problem.

Munna is very busy nowadays. He is not busy due to his social work but because of some other destructive work. Although, he never speaks about his work to anybody, not even with Gurmeet. If Gurmeet asks about his business, then he says that it is a surprise for her which she will come to know when the time comes. Till then she should be patient.

The hot weather is at its peak and it is very hard to get out of homes now. In this sultry summer afternoon, there is no hustle-bustle outside. People go out of their homes only if there is urgent work. On such an afternoon, a police car stops before Gurmeet's house. Those sitting inside the car are in civil clothes. Munna comes out of the home and greets them. They enter the house with him. After a while, another police van stops there. Munna welcome them as well. All of them enter the house with Munna. Then onwards they stay at Gurmeet's house for the whole night. They cook, eat and god knows what else they do.

Normally, in high-rise flats, it is not known who is coming in or going from the flat in front of you. Even who lives in it is not known. But in common streets of urban areas, people are attentive to the different/unusual activities in their street or who is coming or going. Therefore, when they see two police vehicles on their street, rounds of whisper go around as to why the Police vehicles are here. Munna comes out of the house and starts clarifying to them that they are his friends. They wanted to meet for a long time. By chance, they have got leave now, and they have gathered here. This message has been spread systematically in the street and the whispers almost hush up now.

The next morning all the ten people come out of the house in a police uniform and decked up with arms. They board the two vehicles with five members in each and the vehicles move further. Geeta calls Gurmeet and tells her all this. She asks Gurmeet to come back today itself as she has some doubts. Gurmeet says that she was visiting her maternal grandmother due to her ill health and now she is almost ok but as there is a small family function here in the evening and they have asked her to stay, she will move from there the next morning and certainly reach Faridabad by the evening tomorrow.

Like yesterday, today also at 5:00 p.m. two vehicles stop near Gurmeet's home one by one. They also seem to be police vehicles. Similarly, 5 people come out of each vehicle in civil clothes. Yesterday's events are repeated. The only difference is that people and vehicles have been changed. Just like yesterday, Munna comes out and explains to the neighbours on his own even without any question from them. He says that they are his friends. One of them is Deputy Commandant in CISF. His battalion has been transferred so their vehicles were passing through this place. We had already requested them to stay with him for one day when they pass from here. So, it is a beautiful coincidence that they are here.

But Geeta becomes more skeptical about Munna. She is unable to understand what she can do now. She calls Gurmeet again and tells her that today also many people are visiting her home she does not find Munna's intentions very good. So, Gurmeet should come back before some untoward event occurs here. Gurmeet assures her that after the function concludes in the night she will leave for Faridabad then only and reach there by tomorrow morning.

By the way, Gurmeet takes part in the celebration despite unwillingness. But she is restless. She feels as if something untoward is going to happen. Many negative thoughts come to her mind in this atmosphere of protest and fear. But there is the compulsion to be a part of the function which she cannot leave and go as this is the desire of her maternal grandmother that she should be a part of the ceremony. Gurmeet cannot share all these with her granny, so she takes part in the function in the evening though unwillingly.

Finally, Gurmeet leaves for her home even before the function ends. She reaches home by 8:00 a.m. Geeta is keeping a sharp eye on all the activities. After reaching home, Gurmeet comes to know that they have left the place before 7:00 a.m. in the morning. This time too, those who had come in civil dress had left her home in CISF uniform with arms (AK 47 guns) early morning. Both the vehicle left at short intervals and Munna also left home after the second vehicle departed.

Three

Parul Patel gets admission to MA, Political Science to get higher education. Although classes are seldom held in Indian colleges, today is the first day at college. On the very first day in the college, she comes to know about the heart attack of Professor D.N. Sharma, head of the department of political science. Professor R. D. Ram, who is supposed to teach the class has also gone to the hospital along with Prof Sharma. The classes will start once he comes back.

Usually, students discuss various topics during the free time but today's hot topic is Professor Sharma who is to retire on the last date of this month i.e. only after three days. A student says that Mr. Sharma did so much for discipline and timeliness in the college. The other student tells that there are many students taught by Prof Sharma who are on the top political positions in different provinces. The Human Resource Development Minister, Home Minister of the country, Education Minister of the state and Chief Minister and Ministers of many provinces are his ex-disciples. He has a very sound understanding of Political Science and he teaches the students in an easy manner. The students cannot forget him and his lessons.

Parul Patel listens to them carefully and asks them how come they know so much about him?

First student: I have been connected to this college for the last four years. I have graduated from here and studied Political Science, so I know him closely.

Second student: My uncle also speaks about him as he was also a student of this college.

Meanwhile, Professor R. D. Ram enters.

Professor: Sorry for the delay. Professor Sharma is our friend and senior and he had a heart attack. Thank God, he is ok now.

Now, the regular classes commence. The first day passes in the introduction, etc. Meanwhile, Parul decides to meet Prof Sharma anyhow, even if not in the college, since he is to retire in 3 days only. She will try to decipher the wisdom of politics and political science from him.

There are some issues which happen at certain times that they become an inseparable part of life and very often they change the condition and direction of life. When a person finds a bit of success towards one's goal in life, one tries to become successful by more dedication. Parul has made politics her purpose and after knowing about Professor Sharma, somehow, she has the telepathy that this is the best time of her life as she has found her own Aristotle or Chanakya. Now, she can weave her future political life. Once, the strong foundation is there, it will not be tough to build the palace of dreams.

Time passes gradually. Prof Sharma is healthy and home now. He has superannuated. Parul has decided to visit him today. It is a holiday. It is about 10:00 a.m. and winter is here with warm sunshine which is pleasant. Parul rings his doorbell. Professor Sharma is reading the newspaper in the drawing-room. His wife opens the door.

Parul: Madam, I am a student of Political Science and want to meet Professor Sharma.

Wife of Professor Sharma: Please come inside.

They reach near Professor Sharma.

Parul: Good morning sir: I have heard a lot about you. People honour you to be a pioneer of Political Science and compare you to Aristotle and Chanakya. I felt like meeting you and I am here.

Professor Sharma: People will say anything. It is their job. What would you prefer, coffee or tea?

Parul: No, thanks sir, I will take knowledge from you.

Professor Sharma: Great! On which topic?

Parul: Sir, I am a student of Political Science. I am headed towards a career in politics and social service is the purpose of my life. So, what shall I focus on and do? What not to do? Please, give some details.

Professor Sharma: See, politics, political science, and social service are three different things. Have you understood these differences and want to make a career in politics?

Parul: Yes sir! But I want to combine them and have a bit of all three. If I have to choose one, I will go for politics and if I am supposed to leave one, I will quit the political science. But would love to combine politics and social service.

Professor Sharma: If somebody combines all the three, it is difficult to go far. If politics and social service you wish to combine, then also you cannot go very far.

Parul: (without hesitation) then I will certainly opt for the politics. I will make my career in it only.

Professor Sharma: Ok. Then the first thing you should know is that nobody is your own in politics. Nobody belongs to your caste, community, class, sect or region. The history is replete with the examples of the son killing his father for power.

Parul: For example?

Professor Sharma: Ajatshatru killed his father Bimbisar. Azadshatru's son Udayan murdered his own father. Ashoka murdered his brothers. Aurangzeb killed his own brothers and jailed his father and many more.

In politics, marriage, festivals, ceremonies, celebrations, and everything should be done keeping in mind its political benefits and utilities. In fact, you should marry also only after assessing the political pros and cons. If politics is your goal, then never go by emotions.

If nobody is your own in politics, then also no one is an alien to you. Maybe you do not like a person, his character or activities personally. You do not like an area, class or religion, but never express your dislike or enmity.

Parul: Why?

Dr. Sharma: Because he can be of use at any stage. Do you know that a time comes when the government collapses due to the absence of just one MP or MLA? You can play the role of kingmaker if you have one or two MPs or MLAs.

Parul: Sir, here reside people of various castes and communities. How to handle them? If we do something for the one, the other gets angry. My family has a little political background; therefore, I know about it.

Professor Sharma: You are leading towards the absolutely right direction. In India, if you are capable of handling caste and religion systematically, you can reach to the top position in politics.

Parul: Sir, what can be done for that?

Professor Sharma: You have to understand SWOT, i.e., strength, weakness, opportunity and threats for this. Then you have to use it keeping in mind its usefulness as per your convenience and show as if it is used for welfare and development in the present political scenario.

Parul: It means I have to show off?

Professor Sharma: It means that it does not matter what you are really doing for the actual development of a caste or community but what matters is their expectations or their leader's expectations from you. Just keep fulfilling that only, even you cannot fulfill it, keep showing or acting that you are dedicated to them. You will keep climbing your political ladder but if you work for their development in real terms, the possibilities are that it may have a negative influence.

Parul: But how?

Professor Sharma: See, if you want to work for the people who follow Islam, you have to bring improvement in the Madrasa system. You have to teach science, math, computer, and English to the kids studying there and improve the condition of their women. There must be an equal civic code for them. But there is no question of the beginning, even if you think about it, all your votes from this community will be divided. The same is with other communities and castes.

Parul: There are many castes and sub-castes among Hindus. How to handle it?

Professor Sharma: Most of the populace in India consists of Hindus, so first of all you have to understand them. Hindus here are divided into various castes and sub-castes and there is a hierarchy among them. It is very interesting that nobody is willing to discard his identity either on a lower rung or higher. You can roughly divide Hindu into four categories the Brahmins (Priest), Kshatriyas (Soldier), Vaishya (Merchant) and Shudras (Workers) varnas. The concept of the untouchable does not come from Hinduism. There is no such mention in Rigveda. Actually, the first-ever mention of the untouchable is found in Buddhist scripture 'Anguttar Nikay'. For the time being, the untouchables are categorised as Shudras.

The greatest weakness of the Brahmins is there self-pride and self-respect. Even if you do not feed them properly, just give them respect and they will remain your slave. Never ever try to insult them even by mistake, otherwise, a great empire like the Nanda Dynasty, to which a warrior like Alexander could not dare to fight, can be destroyed by them. From the ancient ages, they helped the kings and emperors in building the nation. These Kings and emperors gave them respect and honour as they were mostly educated and intelligent, although they lived life by begging for themselves or their disciples. Either collecting taxes for the king or motivating the society for the welfare of the nation, they have performed their best if treated with respect and history gives testimony to it. During the freedom struggle, right from the Chapekar brothers who were hanged, to Ram Prasad Bismil, all were Brahmins only. An English Civil Servant Grierson has written to the extent that Brahmin's anger is more dangerous than that of a Cobra and normally a Brahmin gets angry only if his self-respect is offended. So, even if you do no good to this class, at least show respect to them.

The second Verna among the Hindus is Kshatriya. They are very proud and arrogant. No one of them treats themselves less than Maharana Pratap. You have to feed their false pride only. Akbar was successful due to them. But never ever compare them to Mansingh by mistake. You have to call them chivalrous like Maharana Pratap, Rana Sanga, and descendants of Rana Kumbha. They will serve you honestly. If needed, they will dig the foundation of their destruction themselves, as Mughals made them do. The Mughals usurped their states, dethroned them and made them their servants and mansabdars. They sent them very far from their homes where nobody knew or honoured them, for example, if they wear from Jaipur, they were sent to Kabul. Moreover, the Mughals established relations with them but always satiated their false ego. So, never put a question on their pride and ego.

The third Varna is Vaishyas. This is the most affluent class in India. From the very beginning, the capital is concentrated in their hands. There are possibilities that the situation will remain the same in the coming days. Just like the businessmen in France asked for laissez-faire to the French Finance Minister Colbert, similarly not only Indian but the merchants all over the world are asking for it, i.e. the policy of laissez faire (non-interference).

You have to keep a watch that no gundas, criminals, tax officers or police harass them. This is the most tax-paying class to the government and their success or failure is directly related to the success and failure of the country's economy. They are more affected by economic benefits in comparison to political, social or other benefits. Irrespective of any social, political, economic or national agitation in the country, they are focused on economic benefits only. You have to take care that they do not face any obstruction in economic benefits.

Shudras, their biggest strength or weakness is racial unity. If anyone of this class, from the village level to state level is a bit educated or has established his identity on social, economic or political levels, they become their blind supporters. They see themselves in that person and feel glorified by their names. So, in each state, you have to push ahead some important persons whose surnames shall be Maurya, Kushwaha, Yadav, Ram, Gautam, Paswan, etc. They are very hardworking and believe in their actions. Just be careful that they reap the fruit of their labour and no middleman devours it.

Parul: Sir, please explain some other communities as well.

Professor Sharma: Since I belong to a specific religion i.e. Hindu, I have every right to speak of it and I did so. Also, we enjoy the kind of freedom to have a discussion or discourse on religious issues at any level.

But, remember, you will not have this freedom with other religions. Therefore, if you attend a program or ceremony of other communities or you have to speak about other religions on some occasion, try to speak less, to the point and use written speech as far as possible, otherwise, a small unintentional mistake may anger the people from other community.

Parul: Sir, could you please be specific about the religion though informally?

Professor Sharma: See in India, population-wise, Muslims come next to Hindus only. Their biggest specialty or weakness is their religious unity. Islam gives predominance to religion. To them Allah, Quran, Nabi and religion matter more than nationality or patriotism. It will not matter much what you do for their development or improvement, what you do for the advancement of their religion and propaganda will matter more. In fact, development or improvement works may have adverse effects. So, the policy of religious appeasement will be safest. For example, speak about secularity, build some mosques or Madrassas, add some gazetted holidays on their festivals, arrange some grant for their religion, and give some high posts to their religious teachers or their relatives, etc. until they are in minority. If you accomplish all these about this religion, all their votes will be in your favour.

Parul: Is this rule applicable to other religions also?

Professor Sharma: No, people from other religions like Sikhs, Christians, Jains, Parsis, and Buddhists, etc. are the most educated, understanding, hardworking and economically capable ones. You cannot confound them in religion. They assess what you are doing for their safety, security, development, education, health, and business and their votes depend on these. You have to take care that there is no hindrance in their path of development. The country's International relations also get affected by them to a large extent.

Parul: Sir, last question; why did you say that political science, politics and social service cannot work in correlation?

Professor Sharma: See, in the present scenario political science includes research work, paper, publication, etc. Social service is selfless service of the society as Mother Teresa did. Although, nowadays there is more stress on social work than social service. Politics is what I said before. In politics, a person has to go to any extent for political benefits. Here, your sole goal is the achievement of power, either by hook or by crook. In the contemporary world, if you try to apply Abraham Lincoln's definition of democracy "of the people, by the people and for the people", then you will remain people and will never achieve any political place. Therefore, if you go for social service, politics may weaken or left behind and you will not be able to do justice with political science. That is why all three cannot go simultaneously.

Parul: Now, what is the difference between social service and social work?

Professor Sharma: Whatever it is, you are inclined to social service. Anyway, in social service, old, divyang/physically challenged, orphans and helpless people are helped but in social work, these people are made capable of helping themselves and if possible, others as well.

Parul: Then, where is the problem? Why these three cannot be combined if somebody gives sufficient time?

Professor Sharma: Plenty of time is required for all three. All three are different fields. Politics consists of selfishness and social service is made of sacrifice. You need diligence and dedication to political science. Politics and social service cannot go hand in hand. Take the example of the most disputed issue of reservation. If you wish to do social service and you have the Ministry of SC/ST, you should try to deliver the benefits of the SC/ST reservation to most backward SC or STs living in the forests of Jharkhand, Chhattisgarh, etc. backward Tribes of North East or other most backward SC/ST. These benefits of reservation are not meant for so-called SC/ST living in New Delhi,

Greater Kailash Bungalows or other state capitals or other city's big bungalows, who belong to generations of IAS, IPS or businessman.

But, if you want to give this benefit to real deserving SC/STs, then you have to take back those facilities from affluent ones and mould it to the backward regions and people. But, you will meet with opposition by those affluent and rich SC/ST who do not deserve reservation but are reaping its benefit for generations.

Now, when these stalwarts will oppose you, those backward people for whom you have raised the issue will also support them on the basis of caste and community. As a result, you will lose votes and lag behind in politics. So, politics and social service can be complementary today to a great extent but they are also different and opposite to each other to an extent.

This is the same for reservation on an economic basis. Mandal Commission had proposed for reservation on the basis of caste as economic data was not available at that time. Now, all data is available due to Aadhar and PAN and still, you cannot remove this caste-based reservation to implement it on the basis of the economy so that its benefit reaches the really deserving people.

Parul: Why?

Professor Sharma: Because, first of all, there should be no reservation. You can fetch people to an equal platform on the basis of education and coaching. Still, if you want to give reservation, then do it on a valid formula on an economic basis instead of on the basis of caste. For example, give reservation of 24% to those who have an annual Rs. 40,000/- per capita income, 15% to Rs, 40,000-80,000/- income group, 10% to Rs. 80,000-1,30,000/- income group, Rs. 1,30,000-1,80,000/- income group 6%.

4% to Rs. 1,80,000- 2,50,000/- income group and the remaining should be kept unreserved. This is a formula that can be altered according to need. In this process, the reservation percentage will remain the same 59% except for the caste.

If the reservation is based on the economy, the most backward people of all castes and religions will be benefited from it. But far from implementing, if you give a statement about it, people will be angry and your vote bank may diminish. Although, you are keeping the same percentage of reservation and just facilitating to reach to those who are in true need of it. One greatest gain will be that the caste system which could not be ended by anybody, will suddenly get dilapidated due to the implementation of reservation on an economic basis and this will be certainly in the favour of the country. But, you cannot do this as this may end your political future.

Parul: Sir, I think per capita income in your formula is very low.

Professor Sharma: Suppose somebody is a clerk and his monthly income is 30,000 rupees per month. It does not mean that he will go to the unreserved category. Actually, there are his wife two kids and parents also in his family who are dependent on him. So, his annual income will be three lakhs six thousand and per capita income will be 60,000 only (3.6 lakhs/6). So, he will come in the 15% reservation category. Moreover, it can be changed as per the requirement.

Parul: That's really good, the more backward a person, the more reservation he gets. Then why it will be opposed?

Professor Sharma: Look, the privileged ones who are reaping the benefits of caste-based reservation will oppose it first and the matter will be accorded a political hue. Then those who really deserve caste-based reservations will also accompany them, who could really get benefit if it were implemented on an economic basis. They will be brainwashed that this will be a big injustice. Their children will not get jobs if the caste-based reservation ends and they will feel that their crutches have been snatched through which they have advanced until now. Your vote bank will be destroyed. Your aim was a noble one-to give them strength and self -dependence. This race will weaken the threads of caste and religion and people may think beyond caste and religion. But if you raise such issues, your vote bank will destroy and you will be marginalized politically. A systematic message will be spread against you in the society that you are averse to Dalits and backward people and want to end reservation. So, if you really want to be in politics, think about your benefits only keep away from social service or other issues that may benefit society.

Parul: Why so?

Professor Sharma: Because this is politics where political authority and self-welfare matters more than social service and public welfare for own political benefits.

Parul: These issues are very confusing. They need to be handled carefully. Thank you so much, sir, for imparting this precious knowledge to me. I will keep seeing you in the future also if needed.

Parul is back to the hostel. Christmas holidays are there in a few days during which Parul goes to her home. Gradually, Parul completes her MA (Political Science). Then she enrols for Ph.D. and doing it, she becomes aware of miscellaneous aspects of political science. Although she is not much interested in studies, she keeps visiting her home where she finds political fervour. She is more interested in ground-level politics at home. Meanwhile, once she visits her home during summer vacations, the preparations for legislative assembly elections are on full swing. The discussion about the distribution of election tickets is going on. In the last elections, Parul's father had won State Assembly MLA seat with huge margins so, there is an absolute probability for him to get the ticket and win this time as well. Maybe he is given a ministry this time.

Election preparations are going on rapidly at Parul's place as well. Distribution of tickets is a challenging task for political parties. It has to be kept in mind that the ticket is given to a person who fits in all the criteria of caste, religion, region, language, manpower, ideologies, values and ethics and is a winning candidate while balancing all these in a better way.

Parul's father is a respected man who is honest to a large extent. People trust him. His victory is almost certain. It is necessary for the candidates to remain in the capital of the state during the last phases of the ticket distribution as nobody knows who will remove the other to get himself the ticket. So, he gets ready to go to Lucknow to find what is going on there but Parul asks him not to go as he is not well. She wishes to go herself from his side.

Anyhow, her father agrees to the proposal and Parul moves to the party headquarters asking him to take rest. She returns with the ticket but there is a slight change in it. She gets the ticket for herself in lieu of her father.

It is not clear what happened in the party headquarters but various versions are spread in the public. Somebody says Parul cut her father's ticket for herself. Someone says the party intends to keep elderly people in side-lines and encourage the youth power by giving them tickets. Another view is that Parul is given a ticket to enhance the ratio of women in the legislative assembly and many more. Everyone holds different opinions.

Whatever it is, Parul has her father's total support, and she is elected as the Member of Legislative Assembly with a big margin of votes. Her real political career has begun now. Every day there is a big queue at her home. Somebody wants her to mediate in a quarrel, the other has to present a tender, someone is there for transfer, another for some certificate, etc.

Parul executes everyone's work in a diplomatic way. If a matter is bilateral, she remains alert that the other party does not get angry when she recommends one. In fact, Parul is too far-sighted which decides her political fate. For example, if there is a quarrel between two parties and usually people solve it by themselves, then she is not required there and this makes her entity insignificant. So, she follows this other way and develops a better information system in this field. She is aware of the power of media and information technology in the present age. The individual or political party that uses it in the best possible way will lead better. Otherwise, farmers and labours are the most hard-working and military or army soldiers the most honest people, still, they lag behind economically and politically.

Where ever in her area, there is a dispute or clash, she receives immediate information and her men inform the police station also. As Parul has given instruction the station in-charge immediately comes into action and arrives at the site. He picks the main culprits from both sides and brings them to the police station.

Although, this is a legal matter and comes under the work area of the station in-charge he also depends on MPs, MLAs, and ministers for transfer, posting, etc. nowadays. The station in-charge is just a symbol, the fact is, that it applies to all officers and staff of government and administration who are working on influential posts.

Now, whoever comes first from the group to Parul, she, first of all, exhorts them that she has no charm for politics. She is there only to protect their interests so that no innocent person is punished or accused. They must have paid heed to before doing all this, etc.

A poor person from the village who has never seen police, thana, and court, moreover beaten up by a *gunda* type person is already broken psychologically as the breadwinner of the family has been taken by the police. So, at this moment, if someone is there to help them selflessly, the whole family treats them to be God only.

Then, Parul will call the Thana in-charge right away before the family. She will ask him about the incident and as per instructions, the in-charge will put all the blame on the party in whose favour Parul is speaking. At the end of all this, she will ask the in-charge to free them as they are very special to her. These people are very gentle and I joined politics for them only, otherwise, I am not attached to it. After all this, the police set free the arrested person in a planned manner.

The family is so grateful to Parul and decides to remain loyal to her whole life. They will certainly vote for Parul and thus her purpose is achieved now.

Now, it is the term of the other party which is comparatively strong. In the villages, the news easily spreads about who is approaching whom. The ideology of the Mandal system also applies there, i.e., the friend of a friend is a friend, the enemy of a friend is an enemy and the enemy of the enemy is a friend. Consequently, if one party goes to Parul, normally the other will not approach her. He will go to her opposite party, who also has influence from the government to the in-charge. The Thana in-charge also knows that he has to liaison with all political parties otherwise, it will be tough for him if one is opposition today, comes in power tomorrow.

But, Parul believes that true politics lies in managing both the parties and getting votes from them. As the first party comes to her, she contacts the other one through a mediator and assures them not to worry as their interests will not be ignored by her. She will free their person in police custody. As a true politician, she settles both parties at once. Actually, she has already ordered the in-charge to free the person from the first party before she orders for the second one. This is her mature politics, both the parties let off, votes of the both in her favour and public emotions are in her control.

An order has been issued to the MLAs by a party regarding giving all the contracts for construction works e.g., road, pond, school, etc. to be completed from MLA fund to their own people only. Anyhow it must be done. More efforts should be there to give them all other contracts as they have helped a lot during elections and very soon the next elections will be here, which cannot be won without their aid and support.

In the Central Government, almost all major contracts have gone online on GeM (Government e-Marketplace) and CPPP (Central Public Procurement Portal). So, it is transparent to an extent and there is a rare probability of manual tempering in it. But, state governments still adhere to manual tendering and there is much scope for tampering in it. In fact, this manual system of tendering will remain in the future also as matters like flood, fire, etc. cannot be handled by online tender as they need immediate action.

Now, the contractor meets Parul. She wants to know how is it that only enrolled contractors can get the tenders. What will be her role in it? The contractor says that we need your blessings only, rest will be managed by us. Parul asks again that how is it possible that despite proper tendering the contract will go to the fixed person? Can you explain it to me? The contractor says that we will submit a quotation on abnormally low cost. Naturally, we will be selected as L-1 (lowest one).

Parul: But, if you quote on abnormally low cost, what will be your profit?

Contractor: First of all, we will be L-1 and the contract will come to us. Now, what will happen that concerned engineer and clerk will come to know that we are your persons and so we will reach them? We will give their proper share to them. They will find the difference between our abnormally lowest quoted rate and L-2 which will be normal. Suppose the work is of 3 crores cost and we have quoted 1.5 crores and L-2 has quoted around 3 crores. So, the difference between this 1.5 crores and 3 crores will be balanced by the help of either the engineer or the clerk or maybe both by increasing item wise rate. For example, we have quoted hundred rupees for an item and will add 5 before that 100 and in words, it will be five thousand before hundred. Now, the item that was of hundred rupees will cost 5100 rupees similar things will be done which will give us a profit of lakhs or maybe crores.

Parul: Is it possible in the present day? How can it happen?

Contractor: Yes madam, actually it is very easy. In the previous case, if the quantity is 100, and the cost was Rs. 100, so 100 x 100=Rs. 10,000/- which now becomes 100 x 5100 = 5, 10,000 (Rupees Five Lakhs Ten Thousand). It means an increase of rupees five lakhs in a single item. In the same way, we will add six thousand to eight thousand in other items and the difference between L-1 and L-2 which was 1.5 crores will come down to about one lakh. Thus, the quoted price of L-2 was 3 crores and the quoted price of L-1 will reach up to 2 crores 99 lakhs despite the signature of the tender opening committee from the above-mentioned method.

Parul: But pen, ink, handwriting, etc. will change.

Contractor: Nothing will change madam. The person who has filled the tender form will use the same pen and handwriting to erase the gap between L-1 and L-2.

Parul: What will be your profit?

Contractor: In this process, our company gets the tender, and the profit is of 1 crore 49 lakhs without doing the work.

Parul is quite surprised to know all this but proves herself to be a skilled politician by not giving even a hint of surprise to them.

Her political life keeps going on like this. Since Parul is a beautiful, courageous, laborious, clever and dedicated young woman, she possesses all that one needs to be successful. Her nature and personality are her biggest assets which she moulds as per the situation by sometimes ignoring the big matters and sometimes by giving importance to frivolous issues. At present reaching the zenith of politics is her sole purpose, for which she tries to render her best.

Her parents speak about her marriage but she refuses to do so. She says that she will not marry now. Two types of marriages are in vogue nowadays love marriage and arranged marriage. In the first, love and emotion are predominant and the person marries his/her lover or beloved. In an arranged marriage, the parents search the eligible bride or bridegroom and marry their son or daughter.

But, things are different in the political area as a third type of marriage system is seen here. Here marriages are beyond love or emotion and done for political interests. This is not a new tradition, but it owes its origin to an ancient age. Bimbisar married four princesses who belonged to various provinces for political benefits. The same tradition was followed during the Mughal period and can be found even today here and there.

In a country and province with a deep-rooted social and caste system, where the daughter and to a big extent vote is preferably given in same caste and community, a person thinks a thousand times before marrying to another caste; Parul decides to marry a person from other religion in one stroke.

Nobody knows the true reason behind it. But people keep guessing. Some opine that it is a love marriage, the others say it is a planned political marriage inspired by votes and another version is that she has been trapped by the man of other religion and marrying out of obligation.

Although Parul has decided to marry nobody in her family and society including her parents sounds happy. Even internal happiness cannot be seen on her own face. But her political future will be safer and brighter by this decision for sure. Her political journey will reach new heights. This inter-religious marriage will inflate her vote bank. Even if the wires of her heart are not connected with this marriage but certainly her grip will be stronger on the political clutch.

This marriage is a grand celebration. The Chief Minister of the state, other important Ministers and some Minister from the Central Government attend the marriage. As a seasoned politician,

Parul Patel does not change her religion, caste, name or surname. In a male-dominated society, normally, the girl changes all those after marriage as per the husband, but this does not happen here. Whatever it is, but her vote bank seems to be bigger after this wedding as she has the benefit of the doubt from both communities.

This becomes very clear after the marriage ceremony, that if Parul wins the next elections, she will be included in the cabinet. Her power and influence are increasing by leaps and bounds. She has been included as a member or chairperson in all major committees of the province.

Meanwhile, the five years tenure of the Legislative Assembly has been completed. Parul gets a ticket again from the same place. She once again wins with a huge number of votes. She is included in the rank of State Minister. She is growing day by day.

Each political entity who is either on MP, MLA or people's representative of any kind receives a number of visitors at his/her home. People come with their various problems. One wants a promotion, the other has to get his transfer stopped, someone has to procure liquor contract, and another is there for getting a petrol pump or gas dealership.

Politicians or people's representatives give them time to meet by carefully analysing its importance, their own economic, political or other benefits, and the usefulness of their work and availability of time. They listen to them and take action. Otherwise, they send them back by giving the reason of lack of time.

In the matters where political benefits are involved, the DGP, Secretary, Principal Secretary, Commissioner or other officers are called up in front of the concerned and directed to take action in their favour. The person who has come to the people's representative with much hope is very glad about inside and thinks that his representative is so good to talk to the higher level and instruct to act in his favour. Now, he is truly grateful and promises to remain loyal to them forever.

But, the reality is different. In most of the cases, the call is made to their own Personal Secretary or someone related to them, which is just to make that person happy. This will secure their vote bank for the future. In very rare cases, the call is made to the right person for political benefits only.

One day a jailor comes to meet Parul as he wants to be transferred near his hometown. Co-incidentally Parul is free that day as an appointment has been cancelled for the day. She has a detailed discussion with him on jail related topics. The working of the department, the way prisoners live or improvements to be done, all the topics are there, to be advised by the Jailor. He suggests about prisoner's food, maintenance and remuneration for their work and gives important advice to Parul. He says that whether other improvements come or not, at least, one system must be improved. This is the call of the time and natural justice, in fact, a matter of human rights.

Parul: Which system in the jail should be improved unavoidably?

Jailor: Madam! A criminal's spouse must have permission to meet and spend one night inside the jail or outside it in a separate room after a gap of two to three weeks and this must be arranged.

Parul: It means you want them to meet as normal couples in two-three weeks. Then what is the difference between being in jail or outside?

Jailor: See, the crime is committed by a person and he goes to jail. That criminal should be punished but what is the crime of his/her spouse that he/she is devoid of their natural right? I think Jail Department should arrange this every 15 to 20 days for them otherwise, it is a violation of human rights and infringement of natural justice for the person who has not committed a crime. If you see this seemingly petty issue in a broader aspect, this is one of the basic reasons for the character-related demoralization of the society.

Parul: But how?

Jailor: Madam, as I have experienced during my 25 years of service, I have seen it in the criminals in jail and his/her spouse outside the jail. A person committed a crime either knowingly or unknowingly. He is in jail as punishment but what is the crime of the spouse that his/her natural needs that could be fulfilled by his jailed spouse in a valid manner, is devoid of that?

Do you know madam, it is a bigger crime by us and law in comparison to his crime.

Parul: Is it so?

Jailor: That person committed a crime and has been punished by being put in jail and losing his freedom. But we are committing a crime to him/her and their spouse.

Parul: Which crime and which way?

Jailor: Most of the people in jail have moral turpitude. I have seen that many moral and character-wise strong persons fall morally in jails and they become homosexual and what not. The person who came to the jail just for one crime, in jail he is involved in various crimes and moral turpitude and that I have watched closely.

Parul: Yes, the problem is there.

Jailor: Not only this. Leave the person in jail who is there for punishment. The main problem arises on the other side which is more serious.

Parul: And what is the problem of the other side?

Jailor: Madam, most of the prisoners in jail come there at an average age of 33 years. As per the marriage system here, their wives' average age is about 28 years, normally 5 years younger to him. Now, tell me, what is the crime of that person between 28 to 35 years whose life partner is wrong or criminal? Can you expect a person in modern days who is living out of jail, in a society to live the next 15 to 20 years, i.e., the main household period, without a spouse?

Parul: Yes, this is the problem.

Jailor: Even if he/she wants to live like that, there will be many out there to entrap them. So, the spouse living out of the jail also is corrupted morally. Who is responsible?

Parul: Our society, legal system, and government all are responsible for this.

Jailor: Their kids also get negatively affected by this.

Parul: How is it so?

Jailor: Suppose a criminal goes to jail at the age of 40-42 years. Most of them are men and the average age of their wives will be between 35 to 37 years. In a developing country like India, normally girls get married off around 18 to 20 years of age in rural areas. They have kids from 22 to 24 years of age. Then what will be the age of those children when their fathers go to prison?

Parul: About 13 to 15 years only.

Jailor: Now, what happens that their mother is just about 35 years and the society and the people look at her with bad eyes? The kids are very much negatively influenced if they hear something foul about their parents at this tender age. These children could be an asset to society but they do not have proper development and they are devastated psychologically and mentally due to their parent's mistake and societal attitude. Gradually, they quit studies and stoop to wrong ways. So, both present, as well as the future generations, are destroyed.

Parul: Really this is very unfortunate. You explained the miscellaneous aspects which usually remain unnoticed.

Jailor: There are some other influences on the society which I have not told you.

Parul: What are those?

Jailor: Madam, I am telling a real story now. Maybe, that will clarify other aspects as well. It is the story of a middle-class family. A girl named Reema was married to a boy Raman with full pomp and grandeur. At the time of their marriage, they were 21 and 25 years of age respectively.

After 2 years of marriage, Raman had a fight with his neighbour for some land. They had physical combat and Raman with a stick hits on the neighbour's head and the neighbour dies due to it. Raman was declared the offender, and he got a life sentence for it.

Rima was just 23-24 at that time. So, some persons started flying around her like bees. During all this, Umesh a relative of Raman who worked in Mumbai and was here on vacation comes closer to her. As Umesh was a relative of Raman, there were no obstructions for him to visit his home. Gradually, they had physical relations. Umesh had AIDS and naturally, Rima also got infected.

As time passed, many people made relations with Rima and the result was that 13 persons in the village had AIDS now. Rakesh, the person whose brother was killed by Raman, was also in that group of people who had AIDS.

I do not know the truth, as to why Rima had physical relations with people, whether she knew or not that she had AIDS. Though some people believe that she knew the fact but did so to destroy those people. Whatever it may be, but the biggest truth is that this was the result of let Rima not meet her jailed spouse. You can see the far-reaching effects yourself. The parents, kids, and relatives of those 13 people suffered badly as they were the breadwinners of their families. The human resource and economic resources that could be used for the development of the country is now used in running to the hospitals and medicines for AIDS. If you see the multiplier effect of just one incident, many layers of all these families will open.

Parul: This is so unfortunate.

Jailor: I can tell you another related story.

Parul (Interrupting in the middle): No, no, it is enough. I have understood it now. I have some important duties to perform. See you later.

Parul takes jailer's revelations seriously and promises to herself to do her best for their betterment. She also immediately signs his recommendation letter for transfer and hands him over.

Sometimes in state politics, there comes a point that a person is offered higher posts just to sideline him/her. A Minister of the state is worried about the growing influence of Parul and suggests that the Chief Minister make Parul fight election from a Loksabha constituency where their party has never registered a victory.

In the legislative assembly, she is winning with a big margin of votes due to favourable equations but for Loksabha elections, in that particular area of the state, equations for her and the party seem unfavourable. The Minister tells that it seems difficult for her to win in that constituency. If she loses the Lok Sabha election, she will lose her influence also, of which there is more probability. If she wins the election by bad luck, the credit of win will go to the Chief Minister. The party will have one more seat in the Lok Sabha and this problem named Parul will leave the politics of the state and move to the center and the state politics will be safe for us. It means killing two birds with a single stone. If she loses, she will lose her influence and if she wins, she will leave state politics and move to Centre. The Chief Minister also agrees to the Minister's suggestion. Do not know why he is also uncomfortable with Parul's growing influence.

Parul is called in a planned way and a proposal to win for Loksabha elections from a specific area is put before her. They convince her that she is the most suitable candidate to make party win from that area. So, the party high command has decided to give her the ticket for Loksabha elections.

She has also emerged as a clever player on the political scene. When she finds an opportunity, she also puts a condition. She says that she will follow the orders of the high command and if I win and our party forms government, then you have to ensure that I will get the post of Minister in centre also, as I am a Minister in state here.

The Chief Minister says yes to it immediately. He thinks that Parul's win to Lok Sabha, then the formation of government by their party or in collaboration, etc. thing of future but this will solve the problem named Parul for the time being. If she wins, she will go to the national level politics and it will take time to establish her identity there. On the contrary, if she loses it, his chair will remain safe for the coming 5 to 10 years. Her fluttering wings will be clipped after this defeat. She can be removed from the post of State Minister also when the right opportunity comes.

Four

There are few people whom the almighty bless with all the happiness in the world. Dorothy Jones is one such serendipitous soul. She is very beautiful, modest, cultured and intelligent. Recently her father has been nominated as Lok Sabha MP from the Anglo-Indian quota. But the best thing about Dorothy is that she is brimming with the ideas of environmental conservation, climate change and control on the rising temperature of the Earth. She is inclined to save water, forest and animals. She wants to conserve the diminishing fertility of the land and also to make the resources sustainable which are misused blindly in the name of development. Keeping all these in mind, Dorothy has decided to go to America for higher education in the field of environmental science.

There are many institutions in the developed western countries that provide the facility of admission in the integrated courses of Master's degree and Ph.D. at once, which is easily not available in developing countries like India. It means a master's degree and Ph.D. can go hand in hand this saves 3 to 4 years in comparison to the developing countries. It is the law of the nature that whoever makes the best use of the available time on an Institute or nation, goes far ahead in the race of development. This is one of the major reasons behind the advancement of Western countries in the arena of research and development. As they make the best possible use of time. Obviously, Dorothy gets admission in an integrated course of Masters and Ph.D. in a reputed Institute of New York. Environmental science is her favourite subject and the most important thing is that she wants to serve the society and nation selflessly, in this field and not that for name, fame, position and luxurious living. Her intentions are benevolent, the purpose is pious and she has chosen the right means to achieve it. When the purpose and means both are pure, then God also comes to help in it.

Dorothy is dedicated to her studies and research. Dorothy has some other advantages too, for example, traditional wisdom acquired in India and her inclination and tendency to see the flora, water, forests, land, etc. with a divine outlook. Now, Dorothy is equipped with the available updated technique of research in America along with her rich cultural heritage. So, she is scaling new heights in the field of research in Environmental Science by combining her rich knowledge and modern technology, which leads to positive directions every day.

Dorothy meets George and befriends him who stays adjacent to her hostel. George is a student of an integrated course in Master of Economic science and a Ph.D. George aspires to work and earn fame in the field of Economics. He is willing to make a great contribution in this field for the welfare of the majority of the world so that he will be remembered for times immemorial. His research and work must rise to the level that Royal Swedish Academy would be obliged to confer Nobel Prize on him.

Dorothy Jones and George keep on meeting and chatting on various issues. As both are researching on different subjects, so they talk about the paper and Publications, etc. except the research topic. It could be natural of their age, attraction, affection or maybe similarity in ideas, their feelings and emotions for each other increase day by day and they start liking each other.

Dorothy comes to know about things related to America, like knowledge, science, civilization, culture, religion, philosophy, food habits, etc. from George. Similarly, George also acquires knowledge about India and Indian viewpoints related to all these through Dorothy.

Since Dorothy comes from a developing country like India and is studying in a developed country like the USA, she knows all the pros and cons of both the countries in the sphere of research.

During all this, George asks Dorothy about the difference between the research process of developed and developing countries. Why is it that many students from various developing countries of Asian and African continents come to Europe or America for higher education or research? Is it the unavailability of higher educational institutes or advanced research Institutes with updated technology in these countries? At least, China and India are among the advanced economies of the world. These countries must have developed research facilities. Is there any economic, technical, political or any other reason that these developing countries are unable to contribute that much in the field of original or fundamental research on the global level? Why is it that India could not attain a Nobel Prize in the field of fundamental research during the last 70 years? What is the cause of not having registered even one-third number of patents in India in comparison to America although the population of India is three times more than America? What is the reason for India getting less than 3% of the Nobel Prizes in comparison to America?

Dorothy tries her level best to answer the above questions. But her answers are not very satisfactory. She promises George to answer these questions satisfactorily in detail very soon.

Two things are most important in the field of research in any country, first of all, innovative scientific research and second, best publications in renowned journals in which your impact factor is very high. Dorothy is focusing on small innovative researches rather than big research in environmental science. And this has brought success to her. Very soon, her papers start being published in renowned publications. Her paper has been published even in "The Nature". Dorothy has gone far ahead in the field of environmental science and has been established as a major researcher in this field.

Dorothy's guide Daniel is a gentleman. He has helped Dorothy a lot. But, nowadays his behavior has changed a bit. His intentions did not look good. Whatever could be the reason, Dorothy's beauty, youth, decency, her excellent research work, Daniel's misunderstanding or his own weakness, but Dorothy had made it clear to him that she has travelled this far from India, over thousands of kilometers, just for studies and research. If you can make me finish my research, then do, otherwise, I will find an option. Daniel is very professional, so does not want to lose such a talented student. So, he stops harassing Dorothy and focuses on research work only.

Dorothy meets Dr.Thomas who has come to America from India for post-doctoral studies after doing a Ph.D. from there. It feels so good to meet someone from your own country in a foreign land. And if that person is from your own province and city, then the joy knows no bounds. Happiness is enhanced by many folds. Although, this is also true that if the same person lives in our neighbourhood flat, we would not have even spoken to or have been acquainted with them. Anyway, only one who lives in a foreign country may be able to surmise this happiness. What makes Dorothy most happy is that Dr.Thomas could prove to be a better person to answer the questions George asked Dorothy? Since Dr. Thomas has done his Ph.D. from India, he knows all the whereabouts in the research field there. As now he is doing post-doctor all studies in America, so he is aware of the Western research system as well. Therefore, Dr. Thomas is the most apt person to tell about his comparative experience of all the developed as well as the developing countries.

Tomorrow is Sunday, a holiday for all there, Dorothy, George, and Dr. Thomas. They plan to meet at 5 p.m. in the evening George is unable to reach there, due to some urgent work. Dr. Thomas and Dorothy are busy chatting on various issues related to India and America.

Dorothy: You have done a Ph.D. from India and are doing post-doctoral here. What is the difference between the research systems of India and America?

Dr. Thomas: First of all, time is best utilized here, as you are pursuing your masters and Ph.D. at once. You will receive both degrees in just 2 to 3 years. Now, see the example of India. There Master's degree is a 2 years course, which takes about two and a half years until the final results come. Then we have to dedicate more than 4 years to complete our Ph.D. If we combine both, it took us more than seven years to get these two degrees there. Here, you will receive both Masters and Ph.D. degrees in just 3 years. This difference of more than four years in a person's life means a lot. This is the most important point of life when the craze to do something new is at its zenith. In India, you will find some guides who are good by chance, but the maximum of them exploit the student physically, mentally and in many other ways.

Dorothy: What are the other differences?

Dr. Thomas: In western countries, a person comes to the field of research and higher education due to his / her inclination and interest and so, their output is also much better. In developing countries like India, most of the time and most of the persons join the field of research and higher education when they do not find any other option. The reason behind this is that this field takes too much time for career assurance, i.e. while completing Ph.D., your age becomes about 30 to 35 years and still, there is no job guarantee. Obviously, their output is also similar.

Dorothy: means?

Dr. Thomas: It means you are researching here in Environment Science because you have an interest in it. George is pursuing research in Economic science because he is interested in it. You can take my example, after intermediate, I appeared for the medical entrance exam. I also appeared in the National Defence Academy exam along with it but got selected nowhere. Further, I took admission in Batchelor's Degree and appeared in so many competitive examinations like Bank, Railway, and Staff Selection Commission, etc. After graduation, I appeared in civil services and state PCS examinations. If anywhere I got selected even as a clerk, I do not know whether I would have continued to study further or not but certainly joined at the job. I could marry on time, have children and enjoyed my life in a government job. My situation will be identified by a majority of people related to higher education and research in developing countries.

Actually, the situation is even bitterer. If their age is somehow saved through some Quota/reservation, they apply for the post of group D, peon or hangman (Those who execute the criminals sentenced to death) even after doing a Ph.D. Today in developing countries like India, more than 80% of students, professors or scientists who are in the field of higher education and Research have passed through this process. After intermediate, they go through various competitive examinations. After many failures, they continue their studies like master, M Phil, Ph.D., etc. out of compulsion. At last, they join as a lecturer, professor or scientist. Obviously, the research or findings of that research by such students who are not interested in research or higher studies, are also not so fruitful. This is the reason behind India getting less than 3% Nobel Prize in comparison to America, although the population of India is three-time more than America.

Dorothy: It means that maximum people connected to research and higher education in these countries are lacking kindred attachment to research and also lagging behind in talent?

Dr. Thomas: Not at all, India has no dearth of talent. The only thing is that in developing countries like India, the environment for research is not so good. In India and most of the developing countries, examinations for entrance in medical / IIT / Defence Academy, etc., are held after intermediate. All the intelligent students appear in these exams according to their subjects and interest. Most talented among them qualify for the exams. They make their careers in respective fields and those who are not selected, take admission in graduation. After graduation, they appear for Administrative Services like civil services examination. Those who have graduated in IIT medical etc., also appear in civil services examinations. If not selected or low possibility is seen for selection in the Civil Services, most of the students in the developing countries like India get admission in post-graduation and then M Phil Ph.D., etc. and some of them become lecturers professors, scientists or researchers. Recently thousands of Assistant Professors were appointed in the Bihar government. The criteria for appointment was: 80 percent weightage given for marks obtained in matriculation, intermediate, graduation, masters, etc and only 20 percent weightage was given for Interview. You cannot imagine how not so talented candidates were selected for those posts on various reservation quota due to higher marks in academics only. Prime universities i.e Delhi University, Allahabad University, and some State Boards provides comparatively fewer marks to their candidate but some regional universities and boards provide so many marks to their students, due to this instead of talented candidate a lot of below-average candidates have been selected as Assistant Professor.

Dorothy: How are the research facilities there?

Dr. Thomas: Modern technology and expensive equipment are not easily available there like in western countries.

One reason behind it is economical or less money is spent there on research activities. But the money which is spent on it, is also not utilized scientifically in scientific institutions for example, if you need simple chemicals, consumables, glassware, etc., here how much time it may take?

Dorothy: A few minutes.

Dr. Thomas: But, in developing countries, most of the items are not available in the stores. You have to give an indent and then sometimes, there are not found in the budget head and sometimes it may take months to procure the items from the lowest one (L1) company. In that situation, the continuity of the research or its purpose could have been defeated already.

Dorothy: What if a piece of expensive equipment is required?

Dr. Thomas: Then you have to go through a long procedure. First of all, it will be decided if that equipment comes into the priority list of the institute or not. If it comes in the priority list, then the budget head will be checked for availability for the equipment. Then your indent will pass through Finance, Purchase, etc. sections to reach the technical and purchase committee. This committee will evaluate and decide if the permission can be given to buy this equipment on the basis of its utility, cost, specification, etc. If TPC gives permission, then it will be submitted for Directors / Director General/Vice-chancellors' approval. After his approval, the tender will be given. Then pre-bid- conference, technical bid, and price bid, etc. process will lead to the procurement of equipment. After the opening of quotation comparative statement will be prepared and then sent to the technical purchase committee again. Then TPC will see the lowest rate, specification, and requirement, etc. and if the fund is still available, the permission will be given to placing the order. Then the equipment will be purchased and installed if all the situations favor you.

Dorothy: Otherwise?

Dr. Thomas: No, otherwise as it can be stalled at any stage.

Dorothy: This is very harmful to the research.

Dr. Thomas: That is true but there is something more to it.

Dorothy: And what is that?

Dr. Thomas: There are many problems, from the appointment of researchers to the research itself, in the field of research.

Dorothy: What are the obstructions in the appointment?

Dr. Thomas: See, how the appointment is carried out in American and European countries.

Dorothy: In the western countries, the post is advertised, the board will sit for an interview or the interview may be conducted through video conferencing. Your performance will be observed and you will get appointed.

Dr. Thomas: But this procedure is not so easy in India.

Dorothy: Then how the appointment is done there?

Dr. Thomas: Here, in most of the institutes the process of appointment takes about two years on an average.

Dorothy: Why?

Dr. Thomas: In the developing countries like India, in most of the institutes, there are many formalities to be completed before publishing the advertisement, for example, preparing roster, and then counting the vacancies according to the quota, approval from the Director / Director General /Recruitment and Assessment Board/ Ministry, etc. When the post is advertised, the candidates will apply for it after the advertisement is published. The screening committee will be constituted by the Director/Director General/ Ministry, etc. After the closing date. The members of the screening committee will consider it extra work and do screening as per their convenience by taking sufficient time. The list of the candidates will be sent to RAB or ministry for final approval of screening. The RAB or ministry will finalize that list of screened candidates by adding, subtracting or changing the list as per their norms. After this, RAB or ministry will appoint the selection committee. Then the date of the interview will be fixed according to the convenience and availability of the selection committee. At least 21 days will be given for the interview. If everything is ok, the formality of the interview will be completed.

After that, the recommendation of the selection committee will be sent again to the RAB or the Ministry. After the approval, the results will be declared, an appointment letter will be issued and the candidates will be appointed in the field of research and higher education.

Dorothy: Is there not such a provision that after advertising the posts, screening is done quickly and then an interview is taken and research related people are appointed?

Dr. Thomas: There is a much bigger provision.

Dorothy: Means?

Dr. Thomas: It means, in many research institutes like CSIR, there is a provision of in absentia, i.e., if the individual does not appear in the interview and finds him/her suitable for the post, then he/she can be recruited. Moreover, if the post is not vacant, there is a provision of supernumerary appointment. The government is not lagging behind in making provisions. These provisions are present in a country where a clerk is appointed through a three-stage examination by the staff selection commission. These three stages are the preliminary tests, mains and then typing tests. And see, the scientists can be appointed through an interview and in absentia as well. But these provisions are only symbolic and nominal and there are very few appointments done through these.

Normally, all the formalities are completed before the appointment. It is good to go through all the processes of selection but it should not be so time-taking and boring.

Dorothy: Maybe this long selection process is carried on to choose the best ones.

Dr. Thomas: What do you mean? To choose the best ones? If it was so, then why maximum seats are reserved?

Dorothy: What did you say? Reservation! Is there a provision of reservation even in the fields of scientific research and higher education?

Dr. Thomas: Yes, here 59% of seats are in the reserved category. After finishing Ph.D., one is left with two options- appointment as a scientist or a lecturer; as the students have become overage for other jobs by this time. For both jobs, 59% of seats are reserved. It means that more than half of the researchers will possess minimum qualification and if they belong to a particular caste, class, community or economic condition, they will be appointed to the reservation seats even if there are much more deserving candidates in the non-reserved category. Here, caste or class is considered greater than talent for the research.

Dorothy: At least, there should be no reservation in the field of research. If you really want to give reservation, then it should be given in the appointment of the support staff of the Research Institute and not to the person related to research. Because research is such a process that people are inspired by what the person before you, beside you or others, is doing in which innovative way and they are motivated to do more innovative research. But, if they see that more than half of people who have reached there are on the basis of caste or economy and they are lacking in required intelligence for research or they are not dedicated to research, it will negatively influence others also in this arena. A negative chain may be active here which is very harmful to research work.

Dr. Thomas: Not more than half, the reservation is 59%. Moreover, if the circumstances are favorable, then these people can be appointed on other 41% seats as well due to other factors. They can come from any category.

Dorothy: But, in India, there are high profile institutes like ISRO and BARC also exist, which are no less than NASA. They are even ahead of it in some matters. ISRO had sent Chandrayaan 1 to the moon in less than the cost of making a Hollywood movie. Now, they have sent even Chandrayaan 2. How these institutes are performing so well? Is there no reservation in these institutes?

Dr. Thomas: No, there is no reservation in the appointment of the scientists of ISRO and BARC. Neither political interference is there. Recruitments are based upon merit there.

Dorothy: Is there interference in recruitment in the other research institutes?

Dr. Thomas: Of course. See how recruitment is done in Western countries. First of all, it is seen that how many projects you have brought. How much profit can you give to the institute or the university after meeting up your expenses? Are you so capable that if you are given a permanent appointment, you will not prove to be a burden on the institute or the university? You will work in such a better way that the institute will get fame due to your achievements.

Dorothy: And what happens in recruitment in India?

Dr. Thomas: as I have already told you, in India, more than half (59%) recruitments are based on reservations. There are some deserving people in the reserved category also but forget reservation for a while.

Generally, students there cross the age of 30 while completing their Ph.D. The student is then under pressure from the family, society and economically as well. They are pressurized to marry and have children as some of their friends who got selected initially in Staff Selection Commission, Bank, Railway, etc. and got the job, are married on time and even their kids are now going to school. The parents also lose their patience. The researcher also thinks that if he does not get a job in the next 2-3 years, his future can be bleak. The researcher and his family try their level best in a hurry for recruitment as a scientist or a lecturer in a government organization. In this situation, the betterment of the research work is ignored, and the focus is shifted on lobbying, recommendation, caste and political equations, etc. Many times the cases of bribery, lobbying, recommendation, etc. come to the force along with sexual complaints during the recruitment process. Sometimes, it also happens that a particular post is advertised just to cater to the eligibility of someone special and to recruit him only.

Dorothy: Eventually selected and recruited scientists fully devote their time and energy to science.

Dr. Thomas: Never, a person who was moving here and there for a job is suddenly selected on higher grade, huge salary, and facilities and also have a lot of beautiful girls doing research under and along with them, they devote their mind to that direction in maximum cases.

Dorothy: Really! This is very unfortunate. Here, there are many problems in the field of science. Here, it is very difficult to find good scientists in the field of research and even if you find them, it is difficult to keep them.

Dr. Thomas: It is not like that. In India, there are good scientists who are fully dedicated to the research and fair recruitments are also done. But, the whole system needs to be changed drastically.

Dorothy: Now tell me about the autonomy given to the scientific and technical institutes in India, are they benefited by it or not?

Dr. Thomas: In India, research institutes can be divided into two categories. In the first category, there are institutes like ISRO (Indian Space Research Organization) and BARC (Bhabha Atomic Research Centre), which are empowered with full autonomy, whether it be recruitment or the execution of work. Their performance is also before us.

In the other category, maximum research institutes are autonomous bodies under the society registration act of 1860 or some other technical research institutes or universities. In theory, they have full autonomy but the problem lies in the fact that the heads of these Institutes, e.g., Director General / Director / Vice-Chancellor, etc. are not appointed in an impartial and transparent manner. The appointment to these topmost posts is very rarely made in an impartial and transparent way without any political interference. Most of the recruitments are done otherwise and these heads of the institutes misuse this autonomy for their own benefits.

Dorothy: What happens in their recruitments? How is it that the institute heads misuse this autonomy?

Dr. Thomas: Sometimes what happens in the appointment of the heads of Institutes like Director General / Director / Vice-Chancellor, etc.; that an average professor or scientist becomes the DG/Director/ VC, etc. with the help of some indirect means?

Once these average level scientists or professors are appointed as the head of the institute, they find the numerous powers conferred on these institutes in the name of autonomy for the execution of work. They get unending and limitless powers for procurement and recruitment and even to fully influence and change the condition and direction of the research work going on in his Institute according to his own ego and self. They have unriddled power to travel in the country and abroad and have a good time in the name of science. In fact, the autonomy given to these heads of the institutes for science is considered as personal autonomy by these indirectly appointed, head of the institutes and then commences the misuse of the resources of the country in the name of research and science. Who cares about the growth of new researches, science, and technology? Even shame will be ashamed of their deeds.

Dorothy: What happens there? What these heads of institutes do?

Dr. Thomas: In India, from the very beginning, teaching, learning and scientific activities have remained a prestigious profession. But contemporary professors and scientists have started comparing their prestige to the ostentatious status of the politicians and like their social presence, government vehicles, gunners, etc. In this comparison, they find themselves very low. Then these directors,

DG or VCs who are recruited through some indirect efforts, find themselves less privileged than these administrative officers and politicians. Although, they are incapable of understanding the challenges and difficulties of the lives and works of these administrative or police officers or politicians. They are spending their lives happily and peacefully sitting in ACs and aircrafts.

Anyway, the moment they are conferred with the so-called powers as the heads of the institutes, they head into the misuse of that power or autonomy totally. Then the condition and direction of all the resources of the institute are moulded towards this specific person. Some government vehicles and drivers are provided to his spouse and some other to his relatives. The Director, DG or VC will have plenty of official programs and invite more and more high-level officers and ministers as chief guests in his Institute. He will have many photo sessions with them to decorate his home and of course, to upload on Facebook. He will enhance his liasioning at the cost of the resources of the institute and will try his best to achieve higher post and personal benefit.

They are many heads of the Institutions who are not present in their office or Institute even for 10 to 15 days in a month, as they have received the license to roam about more and more in the country as well as abroad. There are many benefits to it. Their to and fro travel, boarding, sight-seeing, etc. is met out through the government fund. Moreover, the get DA or per diem as extra money and since they perform glorious acts as guests, chief guests or the member or chairperson of the selection board of other institutes, they become habituated of carrying extra money as the honorarium.

Dorothy: After doing all this, how can they find time for research?

Dr. Thomas: Till now the research has become a minor or optional subject to them. At the time of research, nobody knew them except some students. Now they have got great opportunities for sharing the stage with high-level officers and ministers regularly. They are published every day in newspapers, magazines, and media. In this scenario, sitting alone in the lab for research seems to be a second-rate work to them.

Dorothy: It is fine if the head of the institute is directly not involved in the research, he must be helping in the condition, direction and research of other researchers for sure.

Dr. Thomas: A scientist or professor whom nobody out of his institute knew, suddenly receives the fame and honor of an institute head, do you think his pride can remain under control? It does not make a difference to those heads of Institutes who are selected on merit. In fact, they feel unnatural and awkward as the head of an institute and some of them quit in the middle and head back to their previous institutes to carry on their research. Since their administrative responsibilities as institute head hamper the research work to be carried in a better way.

But, the average person who becomes the head of the institute, his ego touches the zenith. If a scientist, professor or genuine worker raises a genuine issue at any stage and the head of the Institute takes it otherwise, then his assessment, promotion or research will be harmed to the maximum limit by the head. They do not realize that they were appointed for the service of the nation. Actually, the common notion is that service to the nation has to be done by the soldier standing on the border only. They have been appointed for serving and working for the nation. Normally, working in the country's favor is equated to border security.

The civilians who get a fat salary, use all facilities available and live a luxurious life have been recruited to work for their personal benefit and also to enrich their children. If somebody talks to them about real scientific research, they feel as if a question has been put on their work. So, the real scientists or professors, who are involved in research, have to face many hardships. And those who do not accept defeat, advance in the field of science, technique, and research and reach the topmost position. Otherwise, maximum researchers act as sycophants to their heads of the institutes and speak what they like and complete their service life.

Dorothy: Why so? All the scientists and professors are free and they can pursue research work as per their interest. What is the need for flattery?

Dr. Thomas: it is not so. In India, due to the autonomy conferred on the scientific institutes, their heads treat themselves to be all heads in all the institutes. They can directly recruit "E-II" level scientists and terminate the scientists up to the "F" level. They change the condition and direction of the institute as per their interest.

Dorothy: It is ok that they have powers but it does not mean that the head of the institute should turn selfish. They can spend on chemicals and equipment etc. as they wish. They have full power for it.

Dr. Thomas: You are speaking of selfishness, the Director or DG reaches the zenith of his selfishness when only one or two years are left in him turning sixty. He has already moulded the condition and direction of research to his interest and if he is unable to arrange setting for his selection to the post of Vice-Chancellor, then his frustration comes out on his supporting staff.

It is necessary for the directors to be Vice-Chancellor because he has become a director from the post of Professor, then after turning 60 either he has to retire or if, on deputation, he has to return as the professor and teach the students again. The retirement age of a professor or VC is 65 years in the universities, whereas, in other research institutes it comes to 60 years only.

Dorothy: Is there a difference in the age of retirement for both?

Dr. Thomas: Yes, there is a difference that is why it is more problematic. The only difference between the one who has become a director from professor and the other who has come from the post of scientist is that since the retirement age of the professor is 65 years and if he is on deputation, then after going back to the university as professor, he will serve 5 years more but the second one will retire at 60 years of age if he is not appointed as the VC of some University.

Once a non-deserving person receives power and sovereignty, he becomes habituated of it and does not want to lose it at any cost. Even the presumption of losing it scares them so much that they forget their normal behavior.

As the age of retirement approaches, the one who has become director through unfair means, his heartbeats increase gradually. They shiver at the mere presumption of losing authority. This shivering occurs more to the one who has become director from a professor in comparison to the one who has been director from a scientist. The scientist has assumed from the beginning that whatever be the age of superannuation, he has to retire on that. He became a Director/ Director-General through the blessing of God, so what, if he could not be a Vice-Chancellor. But those who have become director from professor, it becomes very sad as after enjoying power and status with the ministers, they have to return to teach students and sit in the queue of professors.

Teaching and Research have remained great works in India from the beginning. The teacher builds the future of the country through his disciples. A person remembers his teachings throughout life. Even if the forgets the bookish knowledge, he never forgets the honesty, dedication, virtue, truthfulness, service, and help to others taught by the teacher. In life, if he commits a mistake by chance, the picture of the teacher appears before him.

But, in today's modern age, people connected with teaching and research have also forgotten their basic moral values and ethics and give preference to the materialistic glittering world as maximum people do. Probably, this is the reason behind many people connected to teaching and research who could have contributed actively in building the future of the nation through building the character of the students, have quit their pious job and joined this exhibitionistic race. In this process, they take fair or foul means.

Dorothy: One should try to advance in life through hard work and honestly doing one's job. It is not desirable to take unfair means.

Dr. Thomas: You are talking about working honestly and there are some people who use their Institute, its resources and work for their own development only.

Dorothy: What do you say?

Dr. Thomas: Once my guide narrated a story from his office. He was the senior-most scientist in the institute next to the director. The director was a famous university professor and had been recruited as the director of that scientific institute. He was supposed to return to his university after completing his deputation in two-three months. Meanwhile, it came to his mind to invite the president in an all India level program of the farmers to be held at the end of the next month. The big event consisted of more than ten thousand farmers who came from various parts of the country and buy roots of planting material like mint, etc.

Previously, he had invited the Governor of the State, Deputy Chief Minister, Central Ministers, and many officers, but he was not successful to achieve what he aspired. So, this time he thought of inviting the president and get a chance to have some proximity with him as he is the appointing authority of the Vice-Chancellor of the central universities. If somehow he makes him the vice-chancellor of some University, it will be a record. But, then he came to know that the president would not be able to give time on that date, as he was already booked for that date. He will be available only after 25 days, so the fixed date of the program was advanced for 25 days.

Since my guide was the senior-most scientist after the director, he was given the responsibility of calling the committee members of the program of the farmers and forward the date by 25 days. In the meeting, the desire of the director was conveyed. Usually, it is not opposed by the scientists but an administrative officer was invited here by mistake. He inquired about the positive and negative aspects of forwarding the date. The concerned scientists explained that the positive effects will be that if the president becomes a part of this program, it will be popular in the whole country. The negative influence is that the time of the farming of the roots of the Mentha and other plants will pass on and it will cause big economic loss to thousands of farmers. This loss can be estimated to be in crores. In fact, this will not result only in the loss of the farmers only, but it may also make us again, the importer of the mint next year, for which now we have emerged as an exporter.

The administrative officer told that our institute works for the demoralised farmers and for the benefit of the country. We should not do anything to harm the farmers and the money of the country should not go to foreign countries due to import in place of export. It will certainly add to the popularity of our Institute if the president visits here and that will add to our pride but the benefit of thousands of farmers cannot be sacrificed.

The program of the farmers, the process of giving seeds and roots should be done on the last date of January as it has been the practice for the last so many years and because of which our country has become an exporter from the importer for mint and other Agricultural Products. If the President's availability is at the end of February, then other programmes to be held in February and March can be shifted to that date and he should be invited but not this one which is affecting the benefits of farmers and people in general.

Gradually, the other members of the committee also mustered the courage to support the views of the administrative officer. As a result, it was decided to organise the program of the farmers,

Kisan Mela on the stipulated date and time, i.e., 31st of January. After completing his tenure, the director returned to his parent university. The president could not come to the institute, but the administrative officer had to pay the price for sure. His promotion was stalled.

Dorothy: This is totally wrong. It needs to be changed drastically.

Dr. Thomas: You are right but who will improve the situation and when?

Dorothy: It comes to my mind when you talked of improvement that earlier you said that there is a reservation of 59 percent in the field of research. The reservation continues in the field of medicine also?

Dr. Thomas: Yes, there are reservations in the medical field as well. There it is in the entrance exam and in the selection of doctors as well. On both levels, more than 50 percent of seats are reserved. These reserved category candidates can also be selected for non-reserved seats.

Dorothy: I think the most talented students should be selected for the research field at the intermediate level itself. Medical and scientific research fields should be exempted from the reservation. If you truly want to give reservation then give more to the administrative department but remove the reservation from these two fields. Although most of the scientific departments already have autonomy whether it is being used or misused, this has to be seen. All other research institutes must be provided with the same transparency and freedom like ISRO and BARC have. If the recruitment, purchase process and terms of the audit are improved and made more convenient, the research scenario may change positively. In fact, purchase and money spent on chemicals, consumables, glassware, etc. becomes useless as it is not done in stipulated time-frame. If all these items are taken care of only, India will also become a leader in the field of research like all other fields.

Dr. Thomas: It needs a lot of sacrifices and strong political will power.

Dorothy: The problems in the field of research may be solved if recruitments are done on the basis of interest and ability and not out of obligation or recommendation. A separate cadre, Indian Scientific Services should be created like IAS and IPS. The exam should be conducted at the intermediate level. The topmost qualified students should be taught specific scientific course and they must be connected to the research. An integrated course of Masters and Ph.D. must be introduced. As it has already been commenced in some IITs in India, so would not be very difficult. Innovative research and more and more projects should be made the criteria for early recruitment and after some time, all the students who have qualified ISS and have done specific science courses, their appointment should be ensured. The research and medical field should be exempt from the reservation. It is not a tough job as it is not a removal of the reservation, but just shifting from research and medical fields to some other area or if possible, the whole of the research field should be free of reservation.

As a result, the most talented, intelligent students of the country who have a scientific attitude and are dedicated to science and research will come to join ISS. When the intellectuals will come to this field, who are presently adulating the politicians and bureaucrats, will turn to research and this will certainly benefit science, country and that intellectual as well. As a bureaucrat, they focus on a good income, post, and posting and are dependent on the political leaders, but, now they will focus on research as their name, fame and identity will depend on it. India will not depend on other countries for science, technique, and research as talent has never lacked in developing countries like India. As of now, ISRO has become an expert in sending small satellites, in the same manner, India will be rated as a country with fundamental research, applied research and the discoverer of new techniques.

Dr. Thomas: You are right. The scientist there want to send their children to medical/IIT as per their choice after intermediate, otherwise, they want them to settle in a job after a B Tech, from anywhere. It is considered better to settle in a job somewhere than to have stress due to uncertainty in career, in the field of science and research.

If problems like unavailability of talented students, delay in the purchase of chemicals, consumables, and equipments, etc. are solved properly, India can emerge again with setting new records in the field of research, science, and technique and also a country to give new condition and direction to the whole world.

Dorothy: Let us move now. It is too late.

Dr. Thomas: Yes, please.

They go to their respective hostels and promise to meet again.

Five

Gurmeet makes a call on Munna's cell phone to know his location. But, his number is switched off. Geeta and Gurmeet enter the home together but the house is messed up and scattered. Both of them start watching the recordings. After some sporadic activities, they watch the main part of the recording.

A person sitting on the Sofa looks at Munna and says "Moinuddin, what is the position of your plan? Is everything ok? When will we leave in the morning?"

Moinuddin (until now who was known as Munna in the society): "everything is ok Afzal Bhai. Prime Minister's Roadshow is tomorrow at 4:00 P.M. Rahman has reached in the adjacent house of that road today itself. Arms have been planted there one week in advance when the information of Roadshow reached from Prime Minister's office to the Chief Minister's office. As per our calculation, the Prime Minister will arrive near that house at around 4:20 p.m. Rahman will be waiting there to kill the Prime Minister. All of you know, how accurate Rahman is at his gunshots. That is why Rahman was chosen for this excellent job. Believe me that the Prime Minister of this country will be shot around 4:20 p.m. tomorrow. The moment Rahman finishes his work, I will inform all of you on the cell phone and five important places in the four cities of India will be destroyed within 5 minutes. Thus, India will be devastated and helpless before the World."

Afzal: Which of the arms are there?

Moinuddin: A sniper rifle has been placed there. An extra SLR is also put there. Since AK 47 is not suitable for a long-distance shot, I have not placed it there. It was very tough to place a sniper rifle there.

Afzal: What is the position of all other places?

Moinuddin: The best-staying arrangement available near Mumbai Stock Exchange has been provided and arms have reached there. Khurshid's team has already arrived there. He will wait for orders. Everybody will be present in commando uniform with AK 47 and hand grenade in a ready position. Once they get orders, they will destroy the Mumbai Stock Exchange.

Afzal: What about Banaras?

Moinuddin: Qureshi and his team have left for Banaras today in the morning. Now they have reached there safely. Tomorrow morning they will visit their targets and then will do the preparation in their room. After the orders are given, they will come into action mode. They will be divided into two teams. The first team will ruin Banaras Hindu University and the second one will destroy Kashi Vishwanath Temple.

Afzal: When are we supposed to proceed?

Moinuddin: Chandigarh is about 300 kilometers away from here and it will take 6 to 7 hours to reach there. If you go around 8 p.m. or 9 p.m. you will reach there comfortably before 4 p.m.

Afzal: No, we will be out before that as there could be traffic jams, etc. to delay us. So, why take the risk without any reason?

Moinuddin: As you wish.

The other man sitting in the middle, whose name is Shahrukh, says: What is the reason for these scattered attacks, I do not understand. We could harm these Kafir's (who do not believe in Islam) more through a concentrated attack on one city at a time. The whole of the city could be ruined.

Afzal: Look Shahrukh! Those who have chalked out this plan, are much more intelligent than us. We should never doubt them. These several attacks are meant for the total demoralization of India. See if we attack Bombay Stock Exchange, India will be very damaged economically. Its foreign direct investment (FDI) foreign institutional investment (FII), foreign portfolio investment (FPI), etc. will be influenced very much. It will take several years for India to come out of this distress. Try to understand that this may take India back economically at least for 10 years. It is very necessary to do this as India is progressing very fast. According to purchasing power parity, it has already reached the third position after China and America. If we do not take any action, it will soon become the leading country of the world according to the national GDP and we will become helpless.

After the Assassination of the Prime Minister during the roadshow at Ahmedabad, this country will be erased politically. Neither in the present political party nor in this country, there is a leader who can match his calibre. The second thing is that when President J. F Kennedy was assassinated in America, the whole world could not forget this unfortunate event for years. Similarly, it will happen here and the whole world will remember it for years. Also, no other leader of this country will flutter for long and nobody will think about a surgical strike or bhumi pujan for temple.

Varanasi is considered to be the educational and cultural hub of India. If we attack here, it will certainly damage their education and culture and development wise they will come to our level or even deteriorate down. Long ago Bakhtiyar Khilji torched the Nalanda University here, then we ruled here for about 750 years and also Islamized almost half of India. Today if our ISIS becomes successful, then we will permanently rule here and the whole country will be Islamized.

Shahrukh: What will be the result of the attack on Chandigarh airport? it is the riskiest part of the plan. When the Indian parliament was attacked way back in December 2001, the main goal was to attack the Delhi International Airport itself. But, after realising the difficulties in the airport attack, the target was changed to Parliament. Then why do we have this airport target again?

Afzal: As our team is about to attack Chandigarh airport, it will affect Indian tourism badly. Till now they have segregated our country with other countries of the world but after tomorrow, this country which is rising on the world scenario will look weak, segregated and alienated from the rest of the world. All major countries of the world will issue advisories to their citizens against visiting India. Thus, on one hand, it will gradually become aloof from the rest of the world and on the other, it will be attached to us and gradually we will own it.

Shahrukh again interrupts: if we had to attack an airport anyhow and hijack a plane, then some other airport could have been selected. Chandigarh is a joint capital of Punjab, Haryana and union territory Chandigarh, so it is but natural that the security here must be very high. Moreover, it is a city of Sardars and these Sikhs are very courageous and dangerous and this airport is even a defence airport so it is highly safe.

Afzal: There are many more reasons for choosing Chandigarh. First of all, the border is not very far from here and the second reason is that if we attack Chandigarh and hijack the plane, it will have a long term influence as the message will go that such an important city and that too in the proximity of Delhi has attack and hijacking. So, the message will be that Delhi is not far from the reach of ISIS. The third reason is that it is the capital of Haryana, Punjab, and the union territory of Chandigarh. So, even when they come to know about the attack, there will be a state of utter confusion as to who will take action on it. Shall the Chandigarh police take action or CISF and even they will call National Security Guard from Union.

The message will be conveyed to the Central Government and before a suitable reply will come from them, we would have crossed the border and reached a safe place. Through this attack, message will be conveyed that if the capital of three states can be attacked and hijacked, then what can we imagined for other provinces of India. It means that we are ruling the Indian law and order system and the date of the direct action of Jihad is very near now. As far as defence airport is concerned it is highly confusing because it is defence airport but civil aviation is operated here, even the name of this airport is highly confusing at the airport it is written as Chandigarh Airport but outside, in the city everywhere it is written as Mohali Airport. So, we should try to benefit from this entire confusion.

Do you know when in December 1999 Indian IC 814 plane was hijacked from Tribhuvan International Airport in Nepal, then it was landed at the Amritsar airport of India to fill fuel here? Perhaps they also knew that the plane has been hijacked but they could not decide fast, what to do? How to do and who will take action on it? The Punjab Police was directed not to take any action. The Central Government decided that NSG will come from Delhi and take necessary action. Meanwhile, the plane had flown to Lahore and reached Kandahar via Dubai.

Omar (who is sitting in the middle): The plane hijack is very risky but its benefits are tremendous. All our demands were met within Kandahar.

Afzal: Look, F. B Howle, an economist has rightly expressed that profit is the reward of risk. Either it is business or life in general, the amount of profit will increase with the amount of risk we take. Those who took a risk during the Kandahar plane hijack in 1999, were rewarded sufficiently. Tomorrow we are going to take the risk and we will be rewarded more in comparison to them, even we will be in a better position. They were five in numbers, so they hijacked one plane and we are ten in number, therefore, we will hijack two planes.

Omar: At that time, the hostages were released in exchange of Masood Azhar, Ahmed Omar Saeed Sheikh, and Mushtaq Ahmed and sufficient money in place of them. But, now we will not compromise for less than Kashmir because India has removed Article 370 and declared it as a Union Territory. Once the ISIS rule is established in Kashmir, our expansion to the rest of India and even East Asian countries will be much easier.

Afzal: There is another system for that work, I mean bargaining. We have just to finish our job. Once we are successful in our aim, then all will happen as we and our planners want.

Omar: Tomorrow we have to face security personnel here. Let us see how strong they are.

Afzal: They are not so strong. There are several deficiencies in them. The maximum number of policemen and security personnel superannuate even without firing a shot. They do not fire even if required. There are many reasons for that. First of all, they know that if they meddle with us, they are going to be killed without reason and if they kill us by mistake, their whole life is spent in proving that the encounter in which they killed us, was not a fake one. Many political parties, organisations and secular people here will put allegations of fake encounters on him. If one Indian shoots even one of us, a minimum of 21 policemen, army men or other security personnel will be punished by life imprisonment. For this, our people work on a very large scale, either directly or indirectly and they help us in these times. Sheikh Sohrabuddin and Ishrat Jahan cases are such examples.

Our own people support us indirectly but the educated and secular people here help us directly. They raise their voices and run medal return campaign, signature campaign, etc. They blame the government for intolerance. The Member of Parliament, leaders, actors, movie directors and famous advocates here run a signature campaign to avert the capital punishment awarded to the guilty of

Mumbai blast Yakub Memon and sent a letter to the President to stop his hanging. They argued that if one Yakoob will be sentenced to death, every house in India will have a Yakoob. Because of these reasons, security agencies and to some extent the government also is passive here.

At last, the security personnel here think that it is better to close their eyes than mess with us. As if they are not seeing anything. They are not aware of our activities. Here, the soldier who safeguards the national border is called a hooligan by these secular people and those who indulge in stone-throwing are called miss guided youth. As a result, the security agency people here avoid to meddle with us and be more attentive to save their jobs, lives, and families.

Shahrukh: Can you explain our SWOT.

Afzal: Our strength is our religion, Islam which unites and gives the message of oneness i.e. there is one God "Allah", one holy book "Quran", one nabi "Prophet Mohammad", one country "Islamic State" and one king "Khalipha".

Their weakness is the leading people who become highly aggressive for Islam i.e. Actor Farhan Akatar said that "now we have to protest on road", they even posted a map of India without Kashmir which normally we are doing. Actually, such types of leading people must keep patience and show neutrality.

Our opportunity is the so-called secular kaphirs. They help us like they are saying "Bharat Tere Tukade Honge, Insa Allah Insa Allah".

Our threat is China, Israel, and America. Only these three countries are actually aware of our intention for Islamic expansion.

Shahrukh: But why the political parties and secular people here support us?

Afzal: There are many reasons. They think that by helping us, they are helping the minorities and this renders them name and fame through the media. Secondly, there is a practice nowadays in India that they keep mum on killing of even 21 policemen, paramilitary force men, and military jawans but if people like us are hit even by mistake, these secular people make a big hue and cry. They are considered more educated and intelligent here. The political parties support us because they think that by doing this, they will get all the votes from our community. Some people think that by doing this, they have become the patron of secularism as described in the Preamble of the Constitution. Some of them have an agenda that if they contest an election in the future, they will receive all the votes of our community and political party will easily give them tickets and also some are paid ones.

Omar: By the way, who were the people who ran a campaign or supported us against the death sentence of Yakoob Memon?

Afzal: See it was the actor Salman Khan who dared to tweet first to avert the capital punishment awarded to the Mumbai bomb blast accused Yakoob Memon, after Salman Bhai's audacity, film producer Mahesh Bhatt, actor Naseeruddin Shah, MP Shatrughan Sinha, famous advocate Ram Jethmalani, CPM General Secretary Sitaram Yechury, the leader Brinda Karat, Prakash Karat and many retired judges, etc. Who belonged to the elite class appealed to avert Yakoob Bhai's death sentence by signing a letter.

Omar: We are very safe in democratic countries like India.

Afzal: Yes, but not only this, here if someone says that, "India will be divided" or "Give freedom to Kashmir", he/she becomes a hit overnight and is invited as a chief guest in many functions and celebrations. Major political parties support him directly or indirectly and give him candidature for the elections. He/she becomes a superstar and even children here know their names i.e. Kanhaiya Kumar and Khalid.

Shahrukh: It means abusing their Nation and religion gives them name and fame.

Afzal: Not only abusing their country, religion, and culture but admiring our religion is also included in it. Then they become a hit. For example, Barkha Dutt, a female journalist here, gives statement on ladies observing Karva Chauth (fasting for the spouse) that she feels regressive, as these ladies are fasting for long life of their husbands, today in this 21st century, but when the month of Ramadan comes after one month, she says, "happy fasting and feasting". Look, she is a hit there now.

Khalid: It means you can say or do whatever you want to this country, its people, religion, philosophy, and national symbol. Nothing is going to happen to you, on the contrary, you become a star or a celebrity.

Afzal: You are right. You can say anything about the majority of this Nation, the elite class, novel class, secular people and maximum political parties will refer to the Article 19 (1) (a) of the constitution and justify it as the freedom of speech. See another example, 26 January is celebrated here as Republic Day. On the Republic Day, a man Chandan Gupta from Kasganj in UP hosted a tricolour (their national flag) show. Our people killed him. Do you know the version of the seculars and political parties here?

Khalid: What was that?

Afzal: If Chandan Gupta and others know that it was a sensitive area, why did they host a tricolour show there? It was Chandan Gupta's fault that he dared to do a national flag show in such a sensitive area.

Khalid: Does the article (19) (1) (a) of their Constitution provide any such freedom of speech?

Afzal: Not exactly, the secular or intellectual here have interpreted it like this. On the flip side, the truth is that Section 124 (A) of IPC clearly mentions that if by spoken, written, by sign, by visible representation or otherwise, hatred or contempt is disseminated against the government, it is a punishable or culpable act which can lead up to life imprisonment.

Khalid: What is the meaning of a sensitive area?

Afzal: It means the areas with plenty of Muslim population. It is clear that in India, the places with our huge population, the people from other religions can never practice their religious, cultural or national activities with freedom and fearlessness. For example, Durga Puja and Muharram had fallen on the same date. Durga Puja is considered as a big festival of the Hindus. They cannot go for idol dispersal through our population dominant area. In fact, a state government here had postponed the date of idol dispersal due to Muharram coinciding with it. Government orders are issued that Durga puja idol will not be dispersed on Muharram day. Although, later on, the court had cancelled that order.

Khalid: Great, the people here have started considering the areas sensitive in their own country and that too for their own national symbol, religion, philosophy, and culture. It means the situation is very suitable for us.

Afzal: You are right Khalid Bhai. The iron is hot and needs to be hit very hard.

Shahrukh: How can you say that the iron is hot? India was ruled by the Muslims for hundreds of years but these rulers could not convert it into a Muslim nation otherwise, we need not do all this today. Today we have to work twice, in the first phase we are supposed to Islamize them. Then, in the next phase, we have to bring all the Islamized countries under ISIS.

Afzal: Of course, something has been lacking somewhere but so much has been done. Do you know that Afghanistan, Pakistan and Bangladesh of present days were formally a part of India and all the inhabitants here were either Hindu or Buddhist, Jains, etc. during the reign of Chandragupta Maurya, Bindusar, Ashok, etc.

The whole region was ruled from Patliputra, which is modern days Patna. Even some part of Iran was also under India during the reign of Kanishka. Gradually, after the Islamization of these areas, they separated from India. First of all, the Kabul region i.e. Afghanistan was separated. It had come off India long ago during the rule of Jahangir and Shahjahan. Later on, Pakistan got dissociated in the year 1947 on religious grounds as the maximum population in that area were Muslims. After this, Bangladesh was created in the year 1971.

Today, India has more number of Muslims than Pakistan which is a different issue. If you add the Muslim population of Pakistan, Afghanistan, and Bangladesh with Indian Muslims, this could be the largest Muslim populated area of the world. Do you know, what was our population when we come to India? Babar came here with only 10,000 Muslims. Before that, in the year 1192 AD, Mohammad Gauri had left a few thousand Muslims with Qutubuddin Aibak and had gone back home. Meanwhile, a little number of Muslims came here. Just imagine that only 15 to 20 thousand Muslims came to United India and now they are about 70 crores in number.

Shahrukh: 70 crores! But there are only 20-22 crores of Muslims in India.

Afzal: Ok, what about the Muslims living in Afghanistan, Pakistan, and Bangladesh? They were also a part of India earlier and all of them were either Hindus, Buddhists or other non-Muslims. If we add 4 crores from Afghanistan, more than 20 crores from Pakistan, 18 crores from Bangladesh, 20 to22 crores from India, along with some parts of Iran, we may be no less than 70 crores. Prithviraj Chauhan was defeated by Muhammad Ghori in the year 1192 and after that, in merely 850 years we have been multiplied to 70 crores from just 15 to 20 thousand, is it a mean feat?

Shahrukh: what is our position in the global level?

Afzal: See, Islam is the second-largest population in the world.

Christians are leading.

Shahrukh: When shall we reach on the top?

Afzal: What do you mean by when shall we reach? We are almost there. If we count by the number of people who are below 18 years of age, we are already at the top position. But the problem is that our population is mostly concentrated in Islamic Nations, so it is of no use to increase our population in these countries. That is why the speed of increase in our population is less in our countries but it is growing by leaps and bounds in non-Islamic countries.

You can see this in Bangladesh and India. In Bangladesh, the growth rate of the population is normal, i.e.: 1%, whereas in India, our population is growing rapidly, i.e., 2.5% per annum. Globally our population growth rate is 1.8%, whereas, the average population growth rate in the world is 1.1%.

Aslam: Then why are we not migrating on a large scale and targeting each country?

Afzal: We cannot do this. If we do this, these Kafirs could have doubt and it will create difficulties further. Therefore, by expressing our trouble, helplessness and suffering from terrorism, we are migrating as refugees from Syria, Jordan, etc. to other countries. Some educated young men are settling in other countries for a job. All this is done in such an organised way that nobody can doubt our intentions, otherwise, the game may be spoiled.

You know that approximately 85% of refugees in the world are Muslims only. 56 Islamic countries are available in the world but you cannot imagine that if you leave exception, then no refugees can enter into the Islamic Nation. They only enter into non-Islamic nations. It is happening in a highly systematic manner.

Aslam: If according to population, we are in the second position globally, if Allah wills it, very soon we will rule the world. Once the Islamization is completed, we will bring all the Muslims under the aegis of ISIS either by hook or by crook.

Afzal: Yes, we will rule on the maximum portions of the globe in the coming 40 to 50 years.

Shahrukh: But how?

Afzal: As I have already explained, our population has entered or entering into most of the countries in the world in a planned way. For example, if we see Europe, a big number of our population has entered into almost every country in Europe. It is either as a refugee or jobholder there. The number of our people in all the nations, even if not an active member of ISIS, is equal to the Army or police there.

Yes, they are not living a lavish lifestyle there and living as refugees or living their lives anyhow. But what happens is anyone of them arsons their homes, factories or other places and then someone else goes and saves the lives, commodities, etc. from that fire. Now what happens is that the saviour becomes the hero and gets a job, home, etc.? Similarly is the case with theft, rape, loot, etc. One of us goes to commit all these and the other one is there to save the local people from theft, robbery, rape, and fire, etc., in a planned manner.

In most cases, women and children are saved by them and in maximum situations, they help their own people to escape that situation in a systematic way. Thus, by posing to save these Europeans, their women and children, they become the hero. Gradually, they get permanent employment, residence, etc. there through the local people, police, administration and the government. You can see how our community is slowly sitting in Europe in an organised manner and has captured all of Europe. In the first phase, we will settle gradually in these countries, then through rapid population growth, we will use democracy for Islam and ISIS and, you will see how we will dominate in Europe in just 30 to 40 years. Disasters or pandamic like COVID -19 will bemost favourable for our expansion and settlement in ruined Europe. Within 40 to 50 years, all Europe may be ruled by Islamic religious law (Saria) and the ISIS flag will be hoisted there. This is an example that is followed systematically for the majority of Non-Islamic Nations of the world.

Iqbal (who is sitting beside Shahrukh says): In Europe, we are so less in number to date. In 40 to 50 years, our population will hardly reach up to 40 to 50%, then how will it be possible for us to rule Europe? How will Europe be seized by ISIS?

Afzal: Brother Iqbal look! The moment our population reaches 40 to 50% of various European countries, we will use the same formula for Islamization as we did in Iran, Egypt, Jordan, Syria, etc. countries and the whole of Europe would be Islamized one by one immediately. Once the Islamization is finished, then it will not be difficult to bring these converted Muslims under ISIS.

Aslam (sitting beside Iqbal): You have named Iran, Egypt, Jordan, Syria, etc. but these were already Muslim countries, then which formula was applied here?

Afzal: It is not like that. First of all, Islam as a religion was born in the 7th century. These countries are not Islamic ones from the beginning. nowadays, as Europe is a Christian country, just like that, these countries were inhabited by people of various religions. Iran had Parsis as their inhabitants, Christians and other religious people lived in Egypt. Similarly, the Islamic nations of present-day belong to the followers of other religions. We entered these countries, gradually established ourselves there and as our population reached 40 to 50%, we Islamized these countries totally through Jihad and direct action. The people there had no option but to accept Islam or death. Some of them deserted the nation, somewhere killed, and some accepted Islam. So, be clear in your mind that the Islamic nations of the present day are not basically Muslim, they have been Islamized in a planned way.

Aslam: I do not think it to be viable to live as refugees in the area of Kafirs (those who don't believe in Islam) and capture the whole area so soon.

Afzal: Then you have the best example in India itself. In Chakma or Bodoland, our people arrived in the form of refugees, settled there and then we the refugees ruled the area while the original inhabitants killed, left it or whatsoever.

Aslam: If it is so why people do not take caution yet? Why they provide us with shelter?

Afzal: They try to keep our people aloof and segregated as refugees but our people gradually move out of the camps and mingle with the local inhabitants of the country. We get much support in these activities from the poor in our religion who are already residing there. Our relationships and livelihood are associated with them and it helps us to have houses to live in. Gradually, we oust the original inhabitants of the country or start converting them.

Aslam: So, our major issue in these nations of Kafirs or Dar- ul- herv (Non-Islamic countries) is to raise our population up to 40- 50% of the country. The time it will take is important. After 40 to 50%, it will reach 100% in no time.

Afzal: You are right Aslam Bhai. At the time our population reaches 40 to 50% of a country, our hold in the army, police, administration, etc. will be strengthened. We will fix a date for Jehad and will convert the whole country to Islam under direct action. During all these events we try to kill all kafirs except their young women and children. Although, there is an exception like Lebanon where there are 60% Muslims along with 38% Christians. But out of the 60% Muslims here, more than half are Shiites and we Sunnis amount to only 28%. Therefore, Christians have survived here taking advantage of this Shia-Sunni issue.

Aslam: This is not an exception because there also the reality is that they are alive, till we want.

Afzal: Yes, this is the reason behind the survival of Kafir Christians there.

Iqbal (interrupting them): But, why, if they accept Islam easily during Jihad, then what is the need of killing them?

Afzal: it is needed because of several reasons. The first reason is that our people who are still struggling, have survived in adversity and sacrificed their lives, should get authority on the major properties of that country. It is necessary to kill those rich persons for them, even if they are ready to accept Islam. The second reason is that maybe they accept Islam just to show off and later on, they cheat upon us. Why should we take that risk? That is why most of the elderly and young men are killed by us. We will marry their young women and enjoy life. Those who are not beautiful will work as maidservants and we can use them as per our needs. The children will be educated to reading the Quran, Hadith, Kalima and 5 times Namaz in the Madrasa from the very childhood and they will be fully converted to Islam. Then gradually, they will be taken under ISIS.

Shahrukh: What are the steps taken to establish ISIS in countries like India?

Afzal: We are working rapidly on many levels to establish ISIS in India. Right now we are into jihad campaign. We have proclaimed Ghazi, by killing kafirs through such jihad campaigns. We also scare these kafirs to such an extent that they feel insecure in their own religion. It seems to them that their God and religions are unable to protect them and those who are killed in the Jihad campaign, their relatives, neighbours, acquaintances, etc. gradually consider Islam to be a safe religion. Little by little their psychology changes. They are inclined to think that why the religion established after all religions in the seventh century, i.e. Islam, is growing at such a fast pace? Why the other older religions are diminishing, slowly and assimilated into Islam? It is true that according to religion, Islam is in second place in the world population-wise, but as per the population growth rate, Islam is at the top in the world. The moment our religion obtains first place, as per nation and continent, we will convert the whole world into Islam one by one and later on in the Islamic state.

Shahrukh: You speak of Islamization of the whole world. Let us believe you that in the coming 40 to 50 years, all European countries will come under Islamic state, but what is the position of India? It has not been fully Islamized yet. It is still offending the eyes. When it will become an Islamic state?

Afzal: Look, we are working at a fast pace in India in a systematic manner. For example, you can see the population growth here, the educated, urban and rich Momin (believers in Islam) here have only 2-3 children. They want to exhibit that they are educated, have a good job or profession, they are also modern like common Indians but rural or the Muslims from backward urban areas are reproducing 4 to 6 children on an average. Some of them have even 15-16 children. Here also, Some Hinduist organisations are raising questions on it nowadays. Now you can see the rate of growth. Most of the Hindus and non-Muslims have two children, so that their population may keep constant.

Although in the rural areas, some of the backward Hindus or non-Muslims are reproducing more than two children but this also nullifies as many Hindus tend not to marry and many of them lead an ascetic life. Some of them resort to modern thinking and live without marriage and children and then die. But an average Muslim begets 4 to 6 children, it means three times more in their comparison. Then comes the next generation also which is 4 to 6 children, again 4 to 6 in the third generation and India will belong to us in a democratic manner. Then what happened with Iran, Egypt, Syria, etc. will be repeated here as well. It will be named Islamization and also be the most prominent Islamic state of the world. In the future, it may dominate and will be able to fight the only remaining three Kafir nations in the world, i.e., China, America, and Israel consecutively.

Shahrukh: what are the other measures taken here for the Islamic state except for the population growth?

Afzal: On the next level, a number of our youth are joining the modern schools and colleges here except Madrasa in the name of education. They also work side by side and earn some money. Like other children, they do not aim at being educated as they are aware of the fact that someday whole property or assets of the nation will belong to their religion, ISIS and them. Therefore their main purpose is to trap the girls from other religions in their love net. These young men have the advantage of the money they have earned or received from the system. They have sufficient time as they need not study. What they do is spending time and money on the girls from other religions and try to impress them by their simplicity and secularity. They tie sacred thread on their wrist, put handkerchief/scarf on the head or wear a cross in their neck and visit temples, churches, gurudwara, etc. just to prove their religious generosity so that the girls are ready to marry them.

This impacts them in multifarious ways. Once a Kafir's girl is included in our religion, all her children also become Muslims. On the other side, the girl's family is looked down upon by her own caste, religion and family people and the family is shattered. Consequently, the girl's parents either commit suicide or die out before death. Her only brother or sister run to the city after facing harassment of the villagers. Running here and there, sometimes the brother also dies. If there is a sister, she also meets her destiny through the brother of that boy.

This trend of marrying girls from other religions through trap or persuasion is very much nowadays. Although these young men are properly rewarded for this and our system is working for it, in my opinion, it needs to be taken more care of. It is very effective also as it helps increases our population and moreover, it is destroying the next generation of the other religion. So, it doubly favours us.

Shahrukh: And what are the steps taken for the Islamic state on the local level?

Afzal: The work is already on progress on various levels. You must know that in whichever village, the Muslim population has gone up to 40-50%, The villagers belonging to other religions are harassed to such an extent that they run away from that place to save their honour, money, and fame. They sell their properties at dirt cheap prices while leaving the place. At present, the media highlights the name of few such places as Kairana in Uttar Pradesh or Mewat in Haryana. Otherwise, it is a common phenomenon in villages every day. In some places of Bihar and Bengal, our population has gone above 75%. They are Kisanganj, Purnia, etc., to name some of them. In the end, these kafirs are unable to save their honour, money and even fame. As their honour has been lost the victimization of their daughters, money or property through cartels in which they are trapped and sell their properties at a very low price. And imagine, once they run away, what to think about popularity or fame. Let me tell you one interesting fact, our Sufis and saints, along with the so-called generous religious white coloured people, play an important role during all these procedures.

They depict Ganga Jamuni culture and the oneness of Allah, Ishwar, God, etc. and advocate for the equality and good faith of every religion. These kafirs have no doubt about our conspiracy of religious expansion and our people who are related to this work, keep doing their job in a better way. Our fundamental rule is crystal clear, "La ilaha illallah" means there is no one but Allah is only our Khuda and "Mohammad Rasulallah" which means only Muhammad is the messenger of Allah. But, our white coloured people iterate you are the Allah, you are the God out of compulsion. Otherwise, we cannot even imagine to bring on an equal level of a

Kafir's Ishwar or God to our Allah or Prophet. This will be a sin. How can we equate someone with Allah or Nabi? But the thing is that the elephant has two sets of teeth one to show off and the other to chew with. So, the so-called generous people of our religion chant "Allah is you your name, Ishwar is your name, bless everyone with wisdom O God" with the seculars of the Kafir in vain just to show off and thus make our work easy.

Shahrukh: But nowadays, Hinduist organisations are very active here. A prominent person of our religion in the film industry here gave a statement that our children are not safe here. Similarly, a high-profile man retired from a constitutional post also told that minorities are scared here. All this is met with a lot of opposition these days. Some from the film industry have married the daughters of the kafirs and they have Muslim children but they marry second and third time with Hindu women or take help from surrogacy for having more children. It is also opposed here nowadays. They propagate that we are increasing our religious population in a planned manner. These Hinduist organisations are leaking out our plan. This may harm us.

Afzal: Yes, they all harm the Islamic state jointly. Our own high-profile people are more harmful to us than these Hinduist organisations. In fact, these first row people should look softer and save us on time if needed. For other works and population growth, we are here along with others like us.

Shahrukh: If these Hinduist organisations pressurise the government to make a law against those who have more than two children and deny any government help, service and constitutional post to both the parents and children more than two, then it would be very harmful.

Afzal: Not at all, because it may lead to strong debates, discussions, etc. here. The pseudo seculars and intellectuals here may argue that how come the child be held guilty who was born, those who brought him/her to this world, are to be blamed. It may be that the parents will be barred from any government job or constitutional post, but the child who is born in India, cannot be devoid of any rights. This may bring a revolution or maybe the government will rollover. It is impossible to pass this law here. As far as I know about India, this will not deter our mission.

Aslam: Yes these Indians are a different kind of secular people, otherwise, our people came here to rob, exploit and rule them. But now, when the circumstances are in their favour, they still do not misbehave with us.

Afzal: In the beginning, Muhammad Bin Qasim in AD 712, attacked the Sindh region, robbed the city of its riches and murdered the masses. Then there was Mohammad Ghaznavi in the 10th and 11th centuries, plundering and ravaging the land we now call India. He stole from and robbed the famed Somnath Temple. And in AD1398, Taimur Lang attacked the land, robbing of all its riches and executing the masses. Then came Babar who established the Mughal Empire. All of our great marauders and attackers, Ghazis and Momin's declared Jihad at the right moment. Like when Babur sensed that situation would turn disagreeable and inhospitable, he broke all the bottles of liquor right on the eve of the battle of Panipat and addressed his soldiers that winning this land is a Jihad. He did not care whether his opponents were Muslim or not. Many others followed the suit like Sikandar Lodi and Aurangzeb who dealt as much damage as, possible to the Kafirs and their beliefs.

Ahmad Shah Abdali in the year AD 1761 pillaged and plundered so much of the riches and wealth that he would not enforce taxes for years to come. Quite frankly, when it is convenient for us we declare Jihad and loot their riches and rape their daughters. And when in hostile circumstances, we talk of religious brotherhood, harmony, and secularity to bide our time until the situation is favourable for Jihad again. So the elite and the white-collar intellectuals must practice caution and patience or else their undue statements and/

or their works publicly evident for Islamization could work against our interests.

Shahrukh: Oh! How exactly can the elite and white collars of ours hurt our cause? Then what should they do?

Afzal: These high reaching and high born of our religion must practice caution and monitor control over what they state in public forums so that these Kafirs could not spot connections between them and their ancestral marauders like Aabdali, Babar or Taimur. Or else people would notice that even after so many achievements and making their mark in the industry, these guys are still clamouring for their religion instead of the nation. The masses would think if these high born well off guys are like this the common uneducated folks would be worse. They must only project how amiable, accepting our brotherhood is as India has always been quite secular. The people should think that once guys have 8 to 10 children because of illiteracy and backwardness like backward Hindus and other religions. These white collars must emphasize how they have two or lesser children.

Khalid: Yes and either way all the Kafirs from various nations around believe that the increase in our population and even terrorist activities are due to lack of education and widespread poverty.

Afzal: No! Such is not the cause anymore and those guys now know better. There are various institutions and organisation who put out reports, revealing true intentions such as IMF. Those reports state that people serving ISIS are well educated holding posts of engineers, doctors, professors, and administrative posts. And they are well off. Their intention is to ensure Islamic propaganda and the establishment of an Islamic state. For instance, Abu Bakar Al Baghdadi was a Ph.D. The deputy in charge of ISIS in Syria Abu Ali Al Anwari is a professor of Physics, etc.

Shahrukh: Whatever the case be, I feel our progression is quite slow and not even ISIS is coming through its promises.

Afzal: It is not that easy. Do you realise the percentage of minority populations after the establishment of Pakistan in both countries?

Shahrukh: Umm…..?

Afzal: We were a 7% minority in India. Before independence, many Hindus and Sikhs had properties and land in Pakistan hence they decided to settle there. Pakistan had 23% of minorities from the total population. Now the current scenario is that minorities are around 3% in Pakistan and decreasing. This means more than 87% of the minority have been converted into Islam/killed/left Pakistan. They are victims of our whims and if we wanted, we could either convert them forcibly or even execute them. Meanwhile, in India, our population is rising steadily and has crossed more than 22 crores which is more than the Pakistan side. Now, we could demand another Islamic State from India. We must practice caution and strike when the time is ripe. I even have a name already in my mind for our state.

Shahrukh: What is that?

Afzal: Islamistan.

Shahrukh: How exactly did we achieve the drop in minority of Pakistan?

Afzal: The usual modus operandi, our youth marry their daughters, coercion in the name of Jihad. Scare tactics pressurizing them into either leave the land, death or accept Islam.

Shahrukh: Do you think such coercive tactics would be enough for our cause or we would need something more for the future?

Afzal: The majority of Hindu in India, who are known to be peace-loving cowards. They also lack a vision for the future. Others like Jains, Buddhists, Sikhs, and Christians, etc. are not very different from them. So we need not worry. We need to pull up our socks and god-willing we shall achieve ISIS law and sharia in Islamization.

Shahrukh: In India, in the regions we outnumber kafirs, all things must be in order for us?

Afzal: Some districts of regions like Bihar, Bengal, and Assam have our people in more than three- fourths of the population. You can kidnap the daughters of kafirs and even the police would refrain from the investigation. Like a part of Malda, they call it Mini Afghanistan as our people plant opium in that region. The authority cannot do anything about it.

Moinuddin: This is what I have observed about kafirs, they hide their cowardice and call it being secular. They cannot face us.

Afzal: However, some races are there who could oppose our cause.

Shahrukh: Who are those races?

Afzal: The Sikhs come to the mind first. We tried converting their apostles but they would not, even in the face of death.

Shahrukh: If they would have bent their knee, it would have been easier to establish Islamic State and Shariya.

Afzal: Of course.

Shahrukh: What was our course of action then?

Afzal: What we do to kafirs, death! Weird were those people. They would accept death crushed under an elephant's feet but would not accept Islam. No wonder the Sikhs take pride in their Gurus.

Shahrukh: An admirable trait indeed. What are other ethnic groups who could oppose our cause?

Afzal: Like Naga, they are Christians but are unlike other docile Christians of India. The Indian Army has a battalion and Regiment from these people. These cruel beings can devour any creature. If they had their way, they could even cannibalise their enemy.

Shahrukh: So, what is being done to tackle these ethnic groups?

Afzal: We are trying on a bigger scale. We want these races to separate from India. We had made all preparations for a Sikh mutiny in the year 1984 but then Prime Minister would end this in Operation Blue Star. We have been trying again to segregate the Sikhs and sheltering the Pro- Khalistan groups. Organisations like Sikh for Justice are being instigated for this cause. We masterminded attacks in Gurdaspur and Pathankot. The issue seems that Sikhs living in India are not motivated enough for Khalistan as much as those residing elsewhere.

Shahrukh: What about the Naga's?

Afzal: We wanted article 370 enforced in their state which would make it easier to carve out a nation but the Indians spoiled it too. If there was a Christian majority nation bordering Nagaland, it would have made it easier but all are Buddhist nations or states. We are supporting low-intensity conflict and if Allah is willing, it should succeed.

Shahrukh: At what about Kashmir? Why it is not free yet? The situation got worse and now article 370 has been annulled.

Afzal: That does not matter. We have the majority in Kashmir. All we have to do is keep our calm and keep on populating the land. When there will be favourable governance, we shall declare Jihad. All of the regions will come under the aegis of ISIS. First, we drove out the Kashmiri Pandits from their homeland and then populated the region with our men.

UNO asked India for general consensus but India never quite went for it. Because they know that we have the numbers and a true Muslim would support their religion over nation and country. Dogs become "Baphadar" we could not, because we conquered this nation, we are the king of this nation.

Ladakh used to be a part of Jammu & Kashmir before, it mostly consists of Buddhists who are like their Hindu brethren. The primary issue in the region of Jammu. And to further our cause. Rohingya Muslims have been settled at some special places in Jammu. These Rohingya will reproduce and will shoot for around 40 to 50% of Jammu's populace. When that target is achieved, we shall have our way and establish Islamic state.

Shahrukh: How come things were easier in Kashmir? Why not such is possible at other places.

Afzal: Timing my brother. Timing and governance. The Momins (believe in Islam) have always governed the state. It is natural for such a government to side with our cause. Some Buddhists who were displaced from their home in Tibet were not allowed to settle in the Ladakh region while thousands of Rohingya Muslims wear settled in the Jammu Kashmir region, mostly in the Hindu majority of Jammu to alter the demographics. The government has always played a major role in these events, keeping a tab on police and media.

Shahrukh: We thought of Kashmir is a safe option to it anytime from India but the government here removed article 370 and article 35A at once. Moreover, the status of a state has also been snatched from Kashmir and it has been given the status of a union territory. There can never be a situation similar to it was earlier.

Afzal: Yes, the problem is there. When article 370 was applicable here the situation was much different as more and more funds could be extracted from the centre and could be spent on Kashmir and most of the money was spent on our people. The population percentage of Kashmir was just one percent of India and it got 10% of centre total grant. Only because of article 370 and 35A most amounts of 10% grant reached to our jihadi people.

When article 370 existed there, the law was also similar to that. It was like if an Indian married a Kashmiri girl her right to property will end there. Whereas, if a Pakistani man married a Kashmiri girl, then he will also get citizenship of Kashmir. Now, such a law cannot be even imagined there. At that time the government of Kashmir and law worked as we wished. Syed Sala Uddin, the head of Hizbul Mujahedeen has been declared terrorist by the Indian government whereas, four of his sons have been given jobs and high posts in the state government. If it was not article 370, none of his sons could get a government job. If it was not article 370, none of the Kashmiri pandits would have left that place. Until article 370 was there, none of our Kashmiris did any productive work there and still because of subsidy, the poverty level was least here in India (only 4%). Now, Industries will run there, people will work and cannot say, what will happen and how much people will earn by hard work.

It was due to article 370 and 35A that despite being a majority, we took all the advantages of being a minority. We exploited the real minorities and Dalits there in such a way that they become our slaves for generations. Those kafirs could not vote in state elections, their children could not study in Government schools and colleges and they could not get a job in Kashmir. What could they do?

Shahrukh: Cleaning the garbage we spread and our slavery.

Afzal: Yes, but now, all the special rights are gone. Those Dalit kafirs also have all rights as us and they can also vote like us, get a job like us and their kids can study in government schools and colleges. All this menace happened due to the removal of articles 370 and 35A.

But, whatever it is, one thing is in our favour that the Kashmiri populace has a majority of our people belonging to our religion and whenever the government will be favourable or situations will favour us, we will not want article 370 in Kashmir. We will directly create it as another country. Till then, we have to increase our population peacefully in Jammu and Ladakh regions and make people feel our presence sometimes in the meanwhile.

Shahrukh: What is the role of Indian Muslims in establishing the ISIS caliphate in India? I doubt they support their religion over the nation.

Afzal: They have their reasons. They have to live in India with Hindus, their livelihood is dependent upon them. It is not the case that they have not favoured religion. For instance, during the third battle of Panipat when Ahmad Shah Abdali invaded Delhi, the Mughal rulers Shah Alam 2nd looked towards the Marathas for help. However, in the name of religion, all the Mughal and Muslim rulers were united from the region including Nawab of Lucknow and Nizam of Hyderabad. They would then go on to form an Alliance and would first starve and then proceed to kill the Marathas. All fifteen thousand young Marathas were deceitfully killed in the name of religion. Imagine what would have occurred if this event did not take place. In a similar manner, during the partition of India, mostly Muslims supported Pakistan and the Muslim League.

Shahrukh: What about Muslims in the Indian Army?

Afzal: They are not much in numbers if any. The second most senior position in the army is Lieutenant General where our Momin people have served but not at the topmost level. There are Siks, Rajput and Gorkha Regiment in the Indian Army. We might need a Muslim regiment.

Shahrukh: If more Muslims join the army, we just might have it.

Afzal: Yes but Indians would be rather cautious given our history.

Shahrukh: How do you mean?

Afzal: You see once in medieval times, the kingdom of Vijayanagar and Bahmani Saltanat were neighbours in the Deccan part of India. The secular King Dev Rai appointed around ten thousand Muslim soldiers and also allowed the construction of mosques in Vijayanagar. Later during the reign of kings like Krishna Dev Rai, more Muslims wear recruited in the Vijayanagara Army. In the war of Talikotta in 1565, these Muslim soldiers betrayed and shifted to the Bahmani side which lead to a great loss to the Hindu Kingdom.

This same story has been repeated numerous times.

(Moinuddin's cellophane starts to ring....he attends the call)

Moinuddin: Shukraan Allah everything is alright. Now only if tomorrow goes as planned.

Aslam: What care do you have? You will be at a safe place by tomorrow. Will be treated with warmth and comfort just like Dawood and will be designated, Ghazi. Don't know about us, what plans Allah has for us.

Shahrukh: No matter what you say Afzal brother, many Muslims of India consider themselves Indian first then Muslims.

Afzal: Let them be. We have to continue working for our cause. Let the proper Islamization of India occur first, we shall address such people later. I think these people would gladly accept Sharia once it is enforced. The first step is to spread Islam all over the world.

Khalid: Yes, but Muslims like Ashfaq-Ullah Khan and Abdul Hamid have considered nation over their religion, we must not forget this.

Afzal: You all must see this in a positive light. See the revolt of 1857 took place under the leadership of Mughal King Bahadur Shah Zafar II. Therefore the Muslims supported it. Now except for Ashfaq-Ullah Khan, you will never come across any other Muslim who was hanged in the Indian freedom struggle. On the contrary, during that period, we were spreading our religion through Jihad in the Malabar region of Kerala and Novakhali in Bengal, etc. We wear vying for a new nation based upon our religion.

As long as Abdul Hamid is concerned, he was a soldier, and solder is duty-bound to serve his nation and so he did.

Shahrukh: Didn't the Mopla rebellion took place in Malabar quite a while ago?

Afzal: Yes circa 1921, when the Indians were fighting for their freedom and where doing Satyagraha and non-co-operation movement, we wear spreading our religion through Jihad. Although it started as a struggle against the British soon it took the form of our own Jihad. There is nothing wrong or right when it comes to the matter of Jihad. Even kids and little children sometimes as young as five are used in this cause, creating an atmosphere of terror and turning kafirs into Momins.

Jihad is the reason for the spreading of our religion in India. If any country is going through unfavourable circumstances, we as a minority must declare Jihad and spread our word. Thankfully our ancestors did it like this and now that we have the numbers, we can declare it an Islamic caliphate.

Shahrukh: What are the Muslim demographics in various Indian states? What chance does ISIS have?

Afzal: Lakshadweep has Muslim in majority around 97% and has been Islamized, therefore we have around 70% of Muslims in Jammu and Kashmir. 35% in Assam, more than 27% in West Bengal and around the same in Kerala. We also have strong numbers in Bihar.

Shahrukh: So some districts or regions of these states must have Muslims around 40 to 50%?

Afzal: Yes, some regions have more than 80% of our people.

Shahrukh: When we have the numbers in the states of Bihar, Bengal, and Assam, why don't we go the way of Kashmir?

Afzal: See, Kashmir was unique in the sense the government there was ours. So we marked out the people of other religions mainly Pandits. We stuck pamphlets to their homes, to leave or else face the consequences. They would try getting help from the police and administration but all in vain. We took their girls as our third and fourth wives, cut those down who resisted. We constantly terrorised them until they would leave of their own accord. There would be no media or police. All this because the government was formed of our own people. So until we have our own government in the states and proper grip in ministries of a union like home and defence etc we will have to wait. Mohammad Gauri and Babar could not achieve it with wars, we will with our numbers. It is democracy and demographics will decide it.

Shahrukh: We still have the security Agency NIA going after our people and destroying our agenda. It would be nice if we could somehow get it dissolved for targeting us minorities.

Afzal: That is true, on 26th of December 2018 they raided Delhi and Uttar Pradesh and would confiscate many quintals of grenades, launchers, and arms. They foiled our plans. If we were to succeed, we would have made our mark on Kumbh Mela, we would have spread such a degree of terror that all these crores of people would think twice before congregating for this event.

Similarly, the agency would raid Tamil Nadu and would arrest many of our people from the Ansharullah module. But these setbacks would not harm our cause. The American FBI does not recognise us. We change our names and would enlist ourselves in the "Free Syrian Army" and would get training from the American army itself. What can NIA do? As for getting the agency dissolved, it's time will come. The conditions are not favorable now. NIA has been given more power and it can go after cyber and international criminals. You see RAW used to be all-powerful back in the day but once we infiltrated their ranks, we would go on to significantly weaken it. It is all but a nominal agency now.

Khalid: You people are talking about NIA, I think demonetization in India has been most harmful to terrorism and our ISIS activities. Our fake currency job has totally stopped due to demonetization. Now, it is not easy to make duplicates of the new currency notes. Moreover, cash transactions have been controlled and the tight grip of NIA has badly affected our economic condition. Now, sometimes it becomes very difficult to pay even our stone pelters.

Afzal: See, nobody can do anything to one who is helped by Allah. On one hand, India has corrupted our fake currency business through demonetization and on the other, Allah has opened the cryptocurrency market on such a huge level in the world for us. There are more than two thousand cryptocurrencies like bitcoin, etherium, ripple or cardane which are in vogue today of which capitalization is more than 120 Arab dollars. Now, we are earning well under this cryptocurrency.

Shahrukh: If we still had someone like Dawood, this NIA would not bother us.

Afzal: His name still terrorises people. Kareem Lala, Chhota Shakeel, Abu Salem, Tiger Memon, Abdul Latif, and Haji Mastan, etc to smaller property dealers these are all our people. Can you imagine that our Don like Chhota Shakeel was deciding who will become the Commissioner of Mumbai and which Minister will get which portfolio? Even then Prime Minister and Chief Minister used to meet Kareem Lala, still, their Photographs with PM, CM, etc. are available in his house. Even today our smaller property dealers would sometime sale single piece of land to multiple people. These kafirs, if united could seriously work against these dealers but they are divided amongst themselves.

Khalid: Brother Dawood's property was auctioned, what about it?

Afzal: You can guess, no one dared to purchase it. There was one kafir who did try, but he had to forego his caution money, let alone claim the property. The auction was attempted once again but none of the non-Muslim would come forward. In the end, one of our own would claim the property at throwaway prices.

Shahrukh: How coward are these people!

Afzal: They are so timid that our people have been settled in every nook and corner of India. Even there are five Muslim houses in the locality, the azan plays there early morning at 5 am on loudspeaker. Do they have guts to play Ramayana or devotional songs in Lahore or Karachi or any Muslim country at 5 am? In India, whether it is a tourist place, religious place or cultural hub, these people wake up with azan only. Our people are scattered in every corner of India and they make these kafirs listen to azan 5 times a day on loudspeaker so that, when the time comes of islimization, these people know all about azan, namaz, qalma, Quran and Hadis. Once they follow Islam, we will bring them to the Islamic state.

Shahrukh: Why Indians are scared of us?

Afzal: See, this example. Bakhtiyar Khilji robbed and burnt to ashes their international level universities like Nalanda, Vikramshila and Odantpuri in the latter half of the 12th century. Lakshman Sen ruled at that time in Bengal, which he ended and established and strengthened Islam in Bihar and Bengal.

Bakhtiyar Khilji played with religion, philosophy, education, culture, property, and daughter of these kafirs. And the most interesting thing is that despite doing all these, there is a city in his name, Bakhtiyarpur a few kilometers away from Patna the capital of Bihar. These Indians do not have the courage to change the name of this city, It's on his name, who destroyed and looted them.

Shahrukh: What will happen if they change the name of this place? Why are they so afraid?

Afzal: See, this decision will be taken by a leader of some party. If a leader takes this decision, our people will not only oppose it but also kill him and there will be arson. Their houses, vehicles, shops, and crops will be burnt to ashes by us. Then in the next election, he will not get a single vote from the people of our religion and he will be eliminated. That is why these kafirs live peacefully and believe in letting it go the way it is.

Khalid: The Muslims here are simple and sober else we would

have established, an Islamic state long back.

Afzal: Where do you mean?

Khalid: India, where else!

Afzal: Why only India, more than 80% Muslims all over the world are soft-spoken and decent and you should view them in a positive light. You should know that Germans are a decent lot but the Nazis besmirched their name. Due to Nazis in the 2nd world war around 6 crore, people would die and around 1.4 crore were put in concentration camps of which 60 lacs were Yazidis but what could the peace-loving German civilians do? Absolutely nothing! Mostly Chinese are peaceful but what could they do to save lives of their own billions of innocent who were slayed by the communists? Similarly, do you know our population all over the world?

Khalid: How many?

Afzal: One Hundred and eighty crores. If we leave out 80% peace-loving people then those of us leading Jihad would be around 36 crores, more than the total population of America.

Only 19 of us would infiltrate the United States and wreak havoc on the World Trade Centre, killing thousands of Kafirs. Imagine what all of us Jihadis could achieve. What would the 80% of peace lovers do? Absolutely nothing!

Khalid: The attack on the World Trade Centre was first of its kind in 2001. 19 of us would kill three thousand Americans. We 26 of ISIS should at least aim for thirty thousand.

Afzal: Yes, ten of us who will attack Chandigarh Airport, ten in Varanasi, (5 in BHU and other 5 will attack Kashi Vishwanath Temple). 5 will attack Mumbai Stock Exchange in Mumbai while one in Ahmedabad will assassinate the Prime Minister. We have the numbers and the security here is lax compared to America. However, the main target is the plane hijack. These Kafirs will feel the impact of it even worse than death.

Khalid: There have been rumours that instead of proper burials, they want to incinerate the terrorist in a garbage dump.

Afzal: They would dare not think anything on those lines. The terrorist would be given proper "Namaz-e-zanaja", Islamic burials, etc. but nobody would dare call him a Muslim in India. They would claim that terrorist has no religion. Such people like to identify as a secularist and would claim the terrorist was brainwashed and what not, consider the pupils of the JNU. They want freedom for the people of Kashmir. How could you expect such people to burn the terrorist's dead body instead of a proper burial?

Khalid: Hmmm, so it would seem.

Afzal: If they were to implement such a thing there would be less of us willing to wage Jihad as we would then not go to heaven, will not come back on judgment day or Akhirat neither would get the promised 72 virgins. This would be egregious!

Shahrukh: Nevertheless, nobody in the world would do such a thing, let alone India. Those vying for our votes would not let it.

Afzal: Well said Shahrukh Brother.

Khalid: It is late in the night. Should we plan and strategize the tactics about the Chandigarh airport?

Afzal: See, tomorrow we will reach a point nearby the airport between 3 and 4 p.m. We will wait for call from Moinuddin and proceed to the airport thereafter. We have to reach the airport's main gate, where the tickets are checked. We will swiftly cross the boarding area and Security Check. And as they will ask us our whereabouts, we will tell them about a bomb on the airport premises. Meanwhile, Umar will throw a grenade to the other side. And as the security will be distracted, we will enter into groups of five in the boarding queue of whichever aircraft ready for departure.

We will split into a group of two numbers. No matter what. The airport is busiest at that time. The four-five of us with Pilot training will occupy two planes in groups of two, although the plane will be taken off by the Indian pilots only on gunpoint. We have already reconnaissance of the area and location. Now any doubt?

All in unison: No, the plan is clear.

Afzal: Alright then Moinuddin, serve the dinner. We all shall feast.

Moinuddin proceeds to serve dinner. Umar, Khalid, Afzal, and two others help him.

As Geeta switches the computer off, she exclaims: we must inform the police.

Gurmeet: Yes and save a soft copy for security reasons.

Geeta: Correct.

Six

The election commission declares the dates of the election for the Lok Sabha. Parul plays all her cards of deception-lying, caste, religion, male-female, and language in this election. To the women, she says that if you make a female candidate win it means you have won as I am just your representative. To the men, she says that you are sending your daughter, sister and friend to the Lok Sabha, not me. She does not have more to say to the people from her own caste. She has to just keep a watch if somebody else does not buy their votes. She asks for the votes from the people of her husband's religion by saying that now she is also from the same religion. She buys votes through money, wine and other things from the people of other castes and community.

To win an election, you need to work on two levels, first, you have to extend your vote bank and on the second level, you have to cut their votes and destroy their maximum vote bank.

Therefore, Parul Patel expands her vote bank on the one hand and on the other, she finances to the similar caste, religion and community candidates as when against her opponents, so that their votes get divided. Thus, she ensures her win. After the election on the fixed date, results come in her favour. She defeats the opponent with a huge margin of votes and reaches Lok Sabha. The Chief Minister of the state and his advisor Minister are surprised at her big win but they are happy as their wish has been fulfilled and their chairs are secure now. Whatever it may be, now Parul gets a chance to prove herself on national-level politics, leaving behind the state-level politics.

Sometimes, it seems that all the situations in someone's life become favourable, although there is a probability that the person possesses an art that will not let the circumstances go unfavourable or maybe he/she turns it favourable before it becomes unfavourable through farsightedness. It seems to happen with Parul's as well.

After the Lok Sabha election results, there is no clear majority to the party. In this situation, normally the MPs from small parties are bargained for support and the one who is successful in this manipulation forms the government. Incidentally, Parul's party is included in the government. As per the assurance given to her, she also gets the post of State Minister.

As all other politicians on the regional level have done, Parul has also lined up a few loyal supporters who belong to different castes and religions and accompany her in all right or wrong decisions. They solve various problems of the villagers and also work for turning the vote banks into votes.

A problem has occurred during the last few days. After Parul was elected as an MP, one of her supporters, Shamsher Singh has started opposing her. He wants the candidature for the same MLA seat which Parul is supposed to leave for the Lok Sabha.

The problem lies in the fact that if Parul makes Shamsher Singh the party candidate, her other supporters like Azam Khan, Chhedi Paswan, Paras Shah and few others who are loyal to her and are with Shamsher Singh, will be angry with her. The second thing is that Shamsher Singh has become very strong economically. He has also become powerful in the area as his liquor business and food processing industry are doing fairly well for the last few years. Parul sees all this from a political viewpoint and considers that if Shamsher Singh is made the MLA, he may pose a challenge to her. Moreover, this may convey a wrong message among her supporters.

After pondering over all the facts, Parul decides to get the ticket for MLA from her seat to Shiv Manjhi who is from a scheduled caste. He will remain loyal to her. If he becomes an MLA, he is not capable of challenging her. So, nothing to be afraid or to be challenged and Parul will enjoy all the powers indirectly.

When the party declares Shiv Manjhi to be their MLA candidate, Shamsher Singh opposes it and declares himself to be the independent candidate from there. Parul is assured of the victory of her supported candidate Shiv Manjhi after all political mathematics, so keeps mum during elections but as soon as elections come to an end and her trusted candidate Shiv Manjhi wins, she comes in the action mode again. Shamsher Singh, the rebel should not be left like this, as he can be more dangerous in the future and others can get inspiration from him. He must be taught a lesson.

Parul brings all the evil deeds of Shamsher Singh before law apparently with the help of her other supporters. All his illegal activities like liquor business and adulteration in food items, on which police had closed the eyes till date, now come to the limelight. Moreover, a Dalit harassment case is imposed on him in a few days and he is sent to jail. Now, Shamsher Singh applies all his powers and tricks around the court and gets bail and there is nobody to challenge her from her original place.

Meanwhile, Parul is given the charge of the Minister of State for the Ministry of Industry and Commerce. She fulfils all her duties in a dedicated manner. One day she asks the Secretary of industry, the reason behind the good performance of some public sector undertakings and they are categorised as Navratna and Maharatna, but most of the PSUs are performing in a very poor manner. What is the reason for their poor performance? How to improve it?

Secretary, Industry P.R. Pillai: How to expect a better performance from a PSU which is not established properly or has a proper foundation?

Parul: What do you mean by not being established or founded in the right way?

Mr. Pillai: Most of the PSUs are established by the planning of the Planning Commission. The Planning Commission planned for the industry considering all the aspects of it. Although, now NITI Commission has taken place of Planning Commission and working has also changed but the thing is that whether it is Planning Commission or NITI Commission, it planned to keep in view the availability of raw material, energy, labour supply, reach to the market, proximity to the seaport for export, humidity, heat, etc. The appropriate place was fixed to establish the PSU but what happens in maximum cases that at the time of implementation some powerful Minister or stalwart politician takes it to his own state and constituency and all the planning of the Commission goes in vain.

In such a situation, the established PSU is bound to fail. For example, the Planning Commission suggests establishing a food processing unit or apple processing unit in Himachal Pradesh and plans accordingly but the food processing Minister is from Haryana or Punjab and he gets it established in his constituency. So, will that PSU perform the same as it could in Himachal Pradesh? Similarly, the PSU which was planned for Bihta in Bihar will give the same result if it is put in Bareilly of Uttar Pradesh?

Parul: This is the reason behind the poor performance of PSUs.

Mr. Pillai: Yes this is the major reason, though there are others as well.

Parul: What are those?

Mr. Pillai: Do you know who are the MD, CEO, Chairman or major workforce of these PSUs?

Parul: Who?

Mr. Pillai: IAS officers like me who are never related to any PSU.

Neither are they attached to it. A person who is concerned only with comfort, decorum, welcome, good care or respect as a DM or Commissioner of someplace during his service life, what does he know about the technical issues of the PSU? But the condition and direction of this PSU are handed over to him. Consequently, these institutes do not produce the desired result.

Parul: This is so unfortunate.

Mr. Pillai: Yes, this needs to be improved a lot. Now the location of the PSUs cannot be changed easily but improvements can be made in other possible areas.

Parul: But locals can also be changed if needed.

Mr. Pillai: But how is it possible? This will be a tough task with huge financial implications.

Parul: It can be done by establishing units of these institutions in the areas with most output and the focus has to be put on the new unit in place of original PSU. Moreover, it must be handed over to technically connected, attached and those who can think for its benefit kind of persons in place of the prevalent IAS supremacy. Will this not affect the performance of these institutes?

Mr. Pillai: Certainly it will have a positive effect Madam and their performance will improve.

Parul: Tell me one more thing. Why is it that states like Bihar, Jharkhand, and Odisha are lagging far behind despite having an abundance of natural resources? Why these states have fewer industries than it could have been?

Mr. Pillai: No proper attention has been given to these states or you may say they are left behind knowingly. See an example, there was a policy of Indian Railways in the decade of 1980s that the fare of carrying coal, ore or iron from Ranchi/Dhanbad to Patna was put at par with Mumbai, Tamil Nadu, Ahmedabad, and Surat.

Consequently, the Industrialists considered about the favourable conditions in Mumbai or Ahmedabad and neglected Patna or Bhubaneswar. The Railway and Planning Commission had fixed the same freight charges for the supply of raw material from Ranchi or Rourkela to Patna or Bhubaneswar or to Ahmedabad or Mumbai. Then why the Industrialists would pay attention to Bihar, Jharkhand, Orissa or other backward states? As a result, the states with rich resources like Bihar, Jharkhand, and Odisha remained neglected and other states/ regions developed. Industries were established there and people got employment.

These states who produce and supply the resources, i.e, Bihar, Orissa, Madhya Pradesh, and Chhattisgarh fare far behind and are name as BIMARU states. People from these states roam for work and employment as labourers in these so-called industrial and developed areas of Mumbai, Surat, and Ahmedabad. If the intention of the Government and Planning Commission were good, the freight could have been decided according to distance, as it is done now. If it was so, some industries could have been established there also and development could be seen there. People from these areas could be saved from misdemeanours for work in other cities like Mumbai, Ahmedabad, and Delhi.

Parul: Whatever happened, it was too bad. Anyway, start it from today. Do proper planning and just think about the welfare of the country and not for your IAS brethren or any other state region.

Mr. Pillai: I do not believe in all these things. I have risen above all these that is why I have suggested to you about it. I consider all India as mine and not only this, I believe in the concept of "Vasudhaiva Kutumbkam" the world is one family and accordingly I take the whole world as mine.

Parul: That's great! You go ahead and begin from now only. Give your full support and contribution to change the less performing PSUs into most performing ones.

Mr. Pillai: Sure Ma'am, I will.

Mr. Pillai takes her leave and starts to work honestly. Parul executes his plan but very soon the Lok Sabha tenure comes to an end and the Election Commission declares the dates for election. She is unable to implement the plan in a full-fledged manner so that work remains incomplete. Parul again gets the election ticket from the same constituency. This time the verdict is against her party but she wins. As her party is defeated, she has to sit in opposition.

While in opposition, she has much time at her disposal. Normally, when leaders win from a different seat (Lok Sabha or Legislative Assembly) from their own, they seldom visit that place, so the problems of the people there are not attended. But, Parul is different from them. Whatever be the reason, she has to go far in this political journey or people have voted for her and chosen her as their representative, she roams about in her constituency and listens to people's problems and tries to solve them as far as possible, to fulfill her duties. She meets miscellaneous people during this stint. Once she meets a forest officer who has served in the forest department for 35 years and has retired now. Former forest officer wants proper attention to the forest department and also correct the discrepancies in the forest law.

The forest officer tells Parul that except for small amendments of 1980, 2006 or 2019, even today, the Indian Forest Act 1927 is basically applicable in Forest Department. It needs radical change.

Parul: Which type of changes are required?

Forest officer: There are many but first of all, the right to inherit immovable property from the parent must be given to the tribal people as those living in the urban areas enjoy. As in villages or cities, after the death of the father, his immovable assets naturally go to his son/daughter and he/she can either sell it, give it someone or use it, these tribals living in forests, have no rights on their land. They are residing in the forests for generations but they do not own the forest. They cannot sell it or use its plants and trees for their benefit. Do you know, who is the master of those forests where they have stayed for centuries?

India: Who?

Forest officer: Forest officers and staff of the Forest Department like me who are not attached or interested in forests and who are just doing their job and making money.

Parul: But how is it problematic and what is that problem?

Forest officer: Madam, there are many problems. If you go to the jungles, you can find that on both sides of the roads dense and valuable trees cover just an area of 100 to 200 metres. When you go inside, you will see that all valuable and important trees have been cut and sold despite the surveillance by the forest department. The same applies to wild animals. Due to the government's special attention and strict monitoring, the number of tigers has been increasing in the last few years, otherwise, it was also diminishing.

Parul: Then what measures should be taken to save forests and animals according to you?

Forest Officer: If Government spends only one-third of the money it spends' on forest department and its officers and staff, on tribal people and gives them full right on forests, except cutting trees and killing animals, our forests, trees, animals, water and land could have been safe. The forested area which is 22% now, could have been more than 33%, which is essential for the environment and sporadic problems of Naxalism and Maoism had not even existed and tribal people could have been living a happy life.

Parul: Then why is it that your Forest Department is not working appropriately which the tribal people can do?

Forest Officer: Those who are born and brought up in a forest, it is but natural that truly love the forests and they are attached to it by faith, religion, culture, and devotion. If they are given proprietorship for this forest land, they will keep it safe and the animals as well. Moreover, they will use flowers and fruits and it will give them joy.

But, what is happening here is that the tribal people who are born and brought up and residing there for generations, have no right in the forest and they cannot even pluck a flower or branch. The ownership of their ancestral forest has gone to the people from Forest Department who are not related to the forest even distantly. They are here just to do their job and earn extra bucks by right or wrong means. Actually, the government gives them the right to protection of forests and animals in an organised manner and they use it for their needs and welfare. The jungles suffer and their tribal people are saddened and troubled.

Parul: Ok, this department will remain on my agenda and I will think about it as what can I do for it? Of course, I would wish to have the forest, animals and tribal people secure and happy.

Forest Officer: Sure Madam. This I felt for long and thought to convey it to the right person. Now, I have done it and hope that you will raise the issue of protection of forests and welfare of their inhabitants in Loksabha as opposition and many aspects will come to light during discussions. Later on, in the next tenure of Lok Sabha when you are in government, you can easily bring it as a bill and make a law.

Parul: Let see.

The forest officer takes leave now.

Time does not take long to change. Parul, who was struggling to find her place in state politics for the last few years, is now domineering central politics. Now, stalwart politicians can be seen waiting for her. As a result, she has a stronghold not only in her party but also good relations with other major parties as well.

Now, she goes for campaigning for Loksabha and various

state assembly constituencies for her party. During one of such campaigns for the state assembly election, she meets a religious guru, who has a big influence on the maximum populace of that region. She asks for an appointment to meet him, which she gets and she arrives at his place on stipulated time to get his blessings. Actually, her purpose is to spread this message in the public of that area that the Godman's blessings or vote or inclination are towards Parul's party.

The so-called religious teacher meets Parul for a tete-a-tete, but it was not a natural meeting. He touches her inappropriately but anyhow she controls herself as she has turned a shrewd politician now. In place of giving importance to the matter, she prefers the political interest for which she is here. She asks him to support and bless her party and she will meet him when she is free, as for now, she is not feeling well.

The Godman is happy from within that perhaps he is successful in his purpose and for now Parul has some personal problems. But she will come to meet him when time is appropriate.

For the time being, Parul takes his leave. The election ends and the government is formed. Although her party has to sit in opposition at that state assembly she has targeted that religious Guru. Moreover, the ruling party in the state is not happy with him as he had shown his inclination to Parul's party.

Meanwhile, Parul sets a trap for the Godman and sends a girl to him for blessing in a planned way to expose him. As his inclination was to Parul (her party), the ruling party is already angry and vindictive towards him. So, investigations go rapidly and impartially. It is found that a spiritual guru had disguised his actual identity. The actual name of guru was Amanullah Khan instead of Shri Anshul ji Maharaj. Parul's efforts and activeness show off and today the Guru is fighting for life in jail and waiting for his death as well.

While in opposition, Parul has enough time to work for and promote her party and do planning for a better political life. Although she is fed up from these religious gurus, still politics has its own religion, according to which anything is to be done for political interests. There is no permanent friendship or enmity with any caste, religion, class or community. All is as per the requirement of time.

Today is a holiday. Parul has no engagement or program to visit today. She is at peace after so long. Then comes a teacher Dr. Samar Singh to see her at her residence.

Parul: How are you doctor? Is everything ok? What is the purpose of your visit today? I suppose there is no problem.

Dr. Samar Singh: Everything is ok. I am here to invite you for the foundation day programme of our school next month. I have no personal problems, but the country has many. They must be solved.

Parul: Which problems? The ruling party says that the government and administration are much better now in the country.

Dr. Samar Singh: Long back, despite limited resources, fundamental research was given priority. Today India is one of the major economies of the world, still, there is no focus on fundamental research now. Applied research is stressed upon and fundamental research is way behind. As India was a centre of fundamental research in ancient times, similar inclination should be there at present.

Parul: But what are our fundamental researches from old times?

Dr. Samar Singh: Well, we have done a lot of researches in ancient times and if this could continue in the present age, India could be one of the leading countries in the field of research.

Parul: How and what are those researches?

Dr. Samar Singh: The invention of aircraft as described in "The Ramayana". The invention of the live telecast as you can see its description in 'The Mahabharata' where Sanjay explained the war scene to Dhritrashtra while he was present in the palace itself. The invention of zero is there. The numerals which are used today, i.e., 1, 2,3,4,5, etc. have been invented here as we call it to be the international font of Indian numerals. In the field of astronomy, you have a great astronomer like Varahmihir who had measured the distance between Earth and Moon, which was almost accurate. The technique of surgery and great books like 'Sushrut Sanhita' and 'Charak Sanhita' were here in the field of Medical Science. Nagarjuna gave the theory of relativity. An English historian A.L. Basham from Europe writes about the Iron Pillar of 5th Century which is situated in the Qutub Minar campus, it was not possible to mold such a heavy and huge sized iron even in Europe before the Industrial Revolution.

Darwin's theory of the origin of life in water first and then its progressive development was already present in India as the first incarnation of fish in water, which is described in 'Dashvtara'. The second incarnation was the tortoise, which can survive on land adjacent to water, i.e. from water to land. The third one being 'Varaha' (pig) which can live on land and also clean the mud. The fourth incarnation was 'Narsimha' i.e., the process of being human from animal, half-human and half-animal body.

The fifth one is 'Vamana' i.e. first small human, the preliminary stage. The sixth incarnation is 'Parsuram' i.e., the man with a hatchet, fully developed troglodyte. The seventh on is 'Ram', the ideal man who follows all rules and regulations. The eighth incarnation is 'Krishna', who is a perfect man with knowledge of arts and knows love, politics, diplomacy, and sports along with rules and laws. The ninth one is 'Buddha' i.e., a simple living person who has left luxuries of life. The tenth incarnation will be 'Kalki' what is it all? Is it not a scientific description of the development of life?

Parul: These are adages. If India had the techniques of making aircraft or telecast, where did they go? Where did they disappear?

Dr. Samar Singh: Any great technique or activity cannot survive without proper support or tutelage by the state. If you go through history, you will find that in 2500 BC Harappa was developed civilization with stadium, seminar halls made with bricks and bathrooms. They had business with Rome and Mesopotamia. They had brick made houses and good drainage systems but after 1000 years in 1500 BC during Rig Vedic ages they lived in mud and grass houses and their economy was based on a preliminary stock-raising system, which was totally opposite to the developed Harappan civilization. They started again from the initial stage and all the developed techniques, sculptures and architecture disappeared totally.

Emergence and decadence are the laws of nature. The thing is that we should be capable of reaching that level again or even above it, once we get an opportunity and situations are favourable. We have done it.

Parul: If it was so, then why this caste system, upper-lower, Shudras and exploitation of untouchables happened which is still being compensated by reservation?

Dr. Samar Singh: Even in so-called developed countries, there has always been a division of proletarian bourgeois, have class-have-nots, capitalist-labourer, feudalist-worker except for India. It means there has always been an exploiter and the other who is exploited.

The exploiter made the underprivileged work by lashing or on the tip of the sword. Even they haunted humans like animals (Africa) and were sold in America for wheat and maize and they were slaves for whole life. But in India, there was a different system. Here, the first description of class division is found in the tenth Mandal of 'Purus Shsukta' in 'Rigveda' where Brahmin, 'Kshatriya', 'Vaishya' and 'Shudra' are described. There we find a description by a student that he is a poet, his father is a doctor and his mother grinds the flour. It means four different Varna's live happily at home performing their duties. It means at that time the right to choose a profession as per your interest and capacity was there, which is equal to the modern-day right to choose profession or employment as depicted in article 19 of the constitution.

Parul: Then how come there developed various castes and sub-castes?

Dr. Samar Singh: You can see, normally a doctor's family has doctor members only. Similarly, a leader's family has leaders, an actor has actors in his family, an advocate has advocates, the businessman has the same profession people in his family, so on and so forth. Today we have constitutional freedom, still, people choose their paternal profession. There are various options today, so what is the compulsion behind choosing the paternal profession? Similarly, it happened in ancient times when a brahmin's family members were attached to education and charity, one who was into security and safety, his next generation did the same, those doing business had their next-generation doing business and the Shudras like barber or farmer had their next generations into the same work.

As far as the freedom to change the caste is concerned, it was always present there. Do you know who Maharishi Valmiki was? The composer of Ramayana, the first epic?

Parul: Who was he?

Dr. Samar: There is a caste named Dom in the present it is a scheduled caste. He belonged to this. Doms still have the surname Valmiki. Maharshi Vishwamitra was Kshatriya, whose main work was in stately affairs and protection. But, the most interesting fact is that more than 80% of the ancient kings were originally from Shudra families.

Parul: How is it possible? Then why the exploitation of the Shudras is so hyped? What is this?

Dr. Samar: See then we have to understand ancient Indian history.

There was no pre-existing caste system in Vedic times. The work they did was the identity of their Varna. In fact, if we see accordingly, this rule applies even today. This followed until the post-Vedic era. When the state ruling system began, Lord Krishna was a Shudra, his maternal uncle Kansh and Jarasandh were Shudras. Normally, those related to the ruling were called Kshatriya, so the elected/made shudra kings were also called Kshatriya because a person was and is identified by his work and not caste. Since Shudras were in the majority, they chose or made kings. This applies even at present. You can see it in case of the prime minister, president, vice president and maximum chief ministers of states.

The founder of the Shishunaga dynasty was the son of Shishunaga and a prostitute. Then his son Kalashok, the last ruler Nagdashak and many other rulers of this dynasty were like this. In the Nanda dynasty, starting from Mahapadma Nand to Ghananand, all were Shudras. Mahapadam Nand had owned the title of 'Sarvkshatrantak' i.e., (one who kills all Kshatriya). He had killed all Kshatriyas then although he did their job himself. After the Nanda dynasty, there came the Maurya dynasty, from Chandragupta to Brihadratha all of them were Shudras. After the Maurya dynasty, there came the Shunga dynasty for a short period. Pushyamitra Shunga, the commander of the last Maurya king Brihadrath killed him and enthroned himself. By caste, he was a Brahmin, but he worked as a Kshatriya as he was Brihadrath's commander.

If we consider by caste, the brahmins ruled India only from 185 BC to 75 BC in the whole history. Whatever we consider it, either Brahman or Kshatriya rule, it was for a very short tenure. After the Nanda dynasty, the other important one was the Gupta dynasty, which was related to the Vaishya family. So, through all the ancient age, if the exception of Shunga dynasty is left out, it was Shudras who ruled the country, which means, India was ruled by Shudras only predominantly.

Parul: But the Kshatriyas also ruled in ancient times.

Dr. Samar: As far as I understand, in ancient history only one major Kshatriya dynasty, Haryak ruled from sixth century BC to 413 BC (about 200 years) except few small and less important kingdoms. Even there is no surety whether they were Kshatriyas or Shudras. During the Mahabharata, era there was such an amalgamation of castes that if you see technically, they were also not Kshatriyas.

Now tell me, who can exploit the Shudras whose people ruled in ancient times? This is the fallacy of history writing. It has been presented like this to divide the Hindu religion.

Parul: What are you saying? It has been depicted in the Smritis that a Brahmin should live in a four-roomed house, a Kshatriya in a three-room house, a Vaishya in two rooms and a Shudra in a one-room house. Is it right? Don't you think it is wrong? Has it been written during the ruling period of Shudras?

Dr. Samar: Yes, madam, this has been written during Shudra's reign. In fact, all or most of the Smritis have been written during Shudra reign, mainly in Nanda and Maurya era. As far as the question of right or wrong is concerned, you have to understand it in a proper perspective. In Smritis it has been written "Janmana Jayate Shudra" i.e., everyone is Shudra by birth. Nobody is born Brahmin, Kshatriya or Vaishya. After birth if you go for teaching-training then you are a Brahmin, if you do defence and protection, then Kshatriya, business or commerce then Vaishya and services like agriculture or physical labour make you Shudra. The houses have been suggested accordingly to suit your economy better.

Parul: Isn't it wrong to fix who will live in a one-room house and who in two?

Dr. Samar: No, now see the other aspect. Presently, the government of India allots government residence to its officers and staff. Group "A" officers are allotted four rooms quarters, group "B" 3 rooms quarters, Group "C" two rooms quarters and peon or MTS gets a one-room quarter. What is this? In Smritis, there is just a suggestion that Brahmins, Kshatriyas, Vaishya, and Shudras should reside in 4, 3, 2 and one rooms consecutively but today's government of India is doing it mandatorily to their group A, B, C and D officers. These are the Brahmins, Kshatriyas, Vaishya and Shudras in the present world. This also applies to the private sector. This is just a matter of understanding how you present the facts and what is the message you tend to give to the public. Similarly, the government gives other facilities. In LTC, group. A level officer is provided with aeroplane and first AC travel, group B with second AC, Group C with third AC and group D with sleeper class. Medical, telephone, newspaper, etc. all facilities are like this. What is this? So, wherever it is written, it should be understood in proper context and then compared to the contemporary world.

Parul: Ok, I agree that ancient age was ruled by Shudras mostly but the Middle Ages belonged to Rajput or Kshatriyas?

Dr. Samar: It is assumed like that but after intense scrutiny, we find that those who ruled in Gurjar, Pal, etc. regions, most of them come under the OBC category today. If they are considered Rajput or Kshatriyas, still you have to believe that India has established its real identity under the leadership of Shudras only. Right from the ancient times to date, whenever the power is in Shudras' hands, India has expanded intellectually, religiously, politically and area wise. The Indian flag was waved unto Kabul and Kandahar in the reign of Shudras like Chandragupta Maurya, Ashoka, and Bindusar. When the rulers become Kshatriyas, this country was divided into small states and feudal and at last, Delhi also slipped from their hands and went to foreign attackers of other religions. Since I am a Kshatriya, I have no objection to accepting this reality.The middle ages, which you have referred to as the period of Rajputs, had witnessed the continuous fall of India. The country was invaded and looted by heretic invaders and its identity was erased. A big part of India has been lost due to their pride and failure. In the present world, it is inappropriate to call a person Shudra and even more if he is occupying a high constitutional post but, the truth exists that even today caste and Varna system exists here. As these people on high constitutional posts say that is why I am saying that if the Shudras did not come in power, then Kashmir must have slipped from us. And what else we could have lost, it is difficult to say.

Parul: Why do you say this?

Dr. Samar: Because if you see the geographical expansion of India on a statistical basis, the situations did not seem too favourable in the last few days. Today it is the only major Hindu country and here itself the existence of this religion is endangered in a very systematic way through differences divisions, castes, and sub-castes. There are some wolves in the form of so-called seculars who want to destroy it in the name of secularism, Dalit and oppressed. But, whenever the power is with Shudras, they have safeguarded and strengthened the country for the next few centuries as Sivaji did.

Parul: The upper castes (Savarnas) have created these sub-castes of the castes here and they have made the Shudras, oppressed Dalit and backward. In other religions like Islam or Christianity, there is only one religion or caste.

Dr. Samar: Our Vaidik scripture Rigveda does not depict any caste or sub caste. Maybe, these castes and sub-castes have benefited some people, but actually, the reason behind these castes and sub-castes is nothing else but expansive affable culture of India. Here, the snake is worshipped in one area as the cow in another. The mountains are worshipped somewhere, the sun and trees in the other. In these various regions the language, ideas, food, behaviour of the people also vary. In ancient times, they often fought against one another. For example, Lord Krishna subjugated Kaliya, the snake, it means those who worshipped the cows, dominated the people who worshipped the snakes. Gradually, all of them reconciled in Hinduism but they could not leave their identities, religious symbols, and their Gods and Goddesses. That is why we find so many castes and sub-castes here. Today we have a democratic constitutional government. You are a public representative and Member of Parliament. Is it possible to make even one person leave his cast identity, what to talk about a cast?

Parul: What do you mean?

Dr. Samar: It means if you ask a Dalit to become a Brahmin or a Brahman to become Dalit, will they follow it? Not at all, then how do you expect that this country which is made of so many castes and sub-castes, has its religion directed by Savarna or some particular castes? Yes, if here also people were included in religion on the tip of sword-like other religions, then everyone would have been of the same caste and their scriptures and methods of worship would have not differed from each other.

Parul: But, here many castes have been put as oppressed and backward. They are never allowed to reconcile in the mainstream otherwise, they would not have been backward.

Dr. Samar: Is it possible to keep a person Dalit, oppressed and backward today?

Parul: No, it is not possible today, but it has been done in the past.

Dr. Samar: If it is not possible today, then how could it happen then? See, we belong to 'Sarve Bhavantu Sukhinah' i.e. 'let everyone be happy' idea and thought, in such a country, how can you say that some people were kept as Dalits and oppressed intentionally? On the contrary, I will say that they ruled here and these upper castes have led them to the modern lifestyle and development in the present age. Otherwise, most of them would have been living aloof in forests like "Sentinelese" in Andaman Nicobar Islands, totally cut off from modern life and culture.

Parul: How is it possible? Who are these "Sentinelese"?

Dr. Samar: India is a vast country. There were many regions from which people were not connected to the mainstream and they were taught to live a normal life and made aware of modern culture, even by risking lives. Going across the sea is considered inauspicious in our religion that is why the whole of India was introduced to normal life and connected to mainstream except some clusters of islands that were Aryanised later on. Brahmins did not consider it pious to cross the sea and visit these islands previously.

There is a scheduled tribe in Andaman and Nicobar Islands called "Sentinelese", which lives like wild animals even in this 21st century and the government is not capable of connecting them to the mainstream. It is prohibited to enter their area as they hunt humans. So, the direction givers of religion did all this in public interest for free, why the government is unable to achieve this even with all its resources today? If Brahmins or upper castes could have reached there also, they could have been Aryanised, much earlier. Even if Dalit or oppressed, they could have received the benefits of ration, water, clothes, medicines, etc. Their children could receive an education. They could get the advantage of SC/ST reservation and could have been MP's and MLA through it today. Tell me who is wrong? These so-called directors of religion are called contractors of religion and cursed by everybody? If all India had not been Aryanized properly, then many people could have been living aloof like Sentinelese. Many of them who are giving direction to the society by becoming commissioner, DM or DCP although by reservation only, could have been struggling in the forests. As far as backwardness is concerned, it is because of their late Aryanization and introduction to modern life.

Parul: This is ok but it could have been better if India also had one caste-like other religions.

Dr. Samar: You can see maximum unity in Islam. Now see this, Islam looks like one religion from outside with one Allah, one Quran, and one Nabi, but, there are many sects, sub-sects and fraternities like

Shia, Sunni, Ahmadia, Sufi, Mujahidin, etc. They have different mosques and cannot read Namaz together. They have the same religion but are prone to kill one another. It is the same with other religions.

As far as Hinduism is concerned, we have 1280 scriptures, more than a thousand castes, more than one lakh sub-castes, numerous festivals, myriad Gods and Goddesses thousands of sages and hermits and hundreds of languages. Still, all Hindus go to all temples and celebrate all festivals jointly and live with peace and complacency. There is no religious difference and anybody can worship the god or goddess of his choice. Where else will you find such freedom?

Parul: Still, there is always scope for improvement.

Dr. Samar: Sure, but the reservation in jobs on this basis is not good. Actually, it is a stigma. First of all, it should be rationalised and then ended.

Parul: The reservation is not a stigma, but a facility given out of remorse. There is no justification behind ending it because it gives an opportunity of growth to Dalit, oppressed and economically backward classes.

Dr. Samar: Madam, as we discussed earlier, people you are calling backward are who those governed and led the country. I will speak about my own class and this will apply to other castes and classes as well. Why economically backward upper castes have been given a 10% reservation?

Parul: Because they are economically backward and they are provided with an opportunity for development.

Dr. Samar: Thanks you did not say that they are also being exploited. What is the need of giving reservation to them who belong to any caste but comparatively less competitive to advance in the race of development? And those who are running fast in the race of development, what is the need of creating hurdles before them? Why are they harassed? Does the government system not need talented people? Why less talented people are promoted through crutches? Real talented and capable people are disqualified even if they fetch more marks, just because their family or ancestors were hardworking and run ahead in the race of development. This is neither fair nor in the interest of the nation.

Nowhere in this world are caste and backwardness prioritized over talent and hard work. There is no such law in the world that gives precedence to those who are backward in place of those running ahead in the race of development. Those who get less marks are given priority on those who get more marks. Talented people are left to poverty and unemployment and less talented people are given reservation in employment just to bring them on an equal platform. There is no other country in the world that snatches more than the 80 percent employment and development opportunities of its common people to bring them on par with poor and backward people. I do not know if the government wants to make the rich poor or make the poor rich or take the country backward.

Parul is shaken a bit but then collects herself and says: "The ancestors of upper caste people have exploited the ancestors of Dalits and underdogs, so the government is making the upper castes repent for that. There is nothing else to it."

Dr. Samar: I have already explained to you whose ancestors exploited whom along with historical proofs. History is interpreted like these facts are misinterpreted for the sake of personal benefits. Those whom you consider exploited, their whole generations have ruled here. Those whom you call backward, they are brought here from their wild lives by risking lives. Despite all, let us suppose that somebody exploited them, but is it ok to take revenge after hundreds of generations and thousands of years?

See another example. Muslims came to this country as invaders. They looted the property, they played with women, religion, culture, philosophy and almost whole country or you can say, they did not leave anything. sisters and daughters of Hindus were forcefully kept in the "harem" of Muslim kings, Nawabs, and landlords. They massacred people here.

This incident occurred much after this so-called Dalit and backward exploitation and it has better and proper historical, archaeological and literally has foreign authors and pieces of evidence to prove it. Shall it be repeated with Muslims in the present? Shall they be given a chance to repent? If something like this is done with them, will it be justified and human? You are talking about the so-called exploitation of Dalits and backward which happened long before. Actually thousands of years ago. Nobody knows or saw what happened with whom? But these activities by Muslims have 'historical evidence, literary, archaeological and descriptions by foreign travellers along with dates and years. So, today, shall we create harems? Do massacre? Is it justified? Can the government think about it? Can it be justified in this age of human rights?

Parul: No, no, this cannot be done. Those times were different. In whatever way, these Muslims came here, but they settled here and have a major contribution to Indian culture and economy.

Dr. Samar: How can you say this? Will any country accept today that an invader, who rules on you, massacres your people, plays with your religion, honour, money and takes your sisters and daughters to their harem, spends your money on eating and drinking and building Taj Mahal for his beloved by using you as slave, and you argue that he is keeping the country's money here itself and contributing to the economy, culture, and architecture of the country?

Parul: No, you are providing an ex parte interpretation of history.

Dr. Samar: I am not describing history ex parte but the government is doing injustice with the right people on the basis of wrong interpretation.

Parul: What is that wrong interpretation of history according to you?

Dr. Samar: See, history mentions that India was discovered by Vasco De Gama in the year 1498. Is it true? This is written in the history that Bakhtiyar Khilji was peacefully passing through Nalanda University along with his soldiers and that culprit Buddhists attacked his soldiers by throwing books on them, so Khilji put the University on fire in self-defence. Is this true? It is mentioned in history that when Alexander invaded India in 326 BC, his soldiers had got so tired that he did not fight Ghananand, the ruler of the Nanda Dynasty. Is it so?

Parul: Yes, what is wrong with this?

Dr. Samar: Was India discovered in 1498? Before that nobody knew India? Did Hwentsang, Itsing, Selucas, and Alexander, etc. not come to India before that? Did India not trade with the various countries in the world, such as Rome, Mesopotamia or Syria? Vasco De Gama came to India via the sea route, the Cape of Good Hope and discovered a new sea route. The whole world knew India beforehand.

Bakhtiyar Khilji was an invader who was on a spree to destroy the religion, philosophy, culture and education system here. So, he burnt to ashes the non-violent Buddhists and their Nalanda University.

In the year 326 BC, Alexander saw that the Nanda Dynasty in India was many times more powerful than him. In those times, Ghananand had six and a half lakh soldiers. So, Alexander was scared and did not fight, as he had already seen the bravery of small kings like Puru here. So, he preferred to save his honour and returned and not due to the reason that his soldiers were tired or they had differences.

But all these facts have been mentioned in history according to one's convenience and we have faith in it.

Parul: Ok, suppose history has been written as per one's convenience, then, you tell me the contribution of the upper castes in the country?

Dr. Samar: The so-called savarna have sacrificed everything for this country and its people. Despite being the most educated and powerful, they spend their whole life in social service.

They never paid attention to collecting riches. Most of the Ancient stories begin with two sentences 'there was a king' (who was normally a Shudra) or 'there was a poor Brahmin' (who is called Savarna nowadays and deprived of the opportunities for development and employment). More than 90% of freedom fighters were from the upper caste. Whether it is a list of the people crucified or the leaders of social, religious or country's movement or those who educated and cultured the people in the country, those who developed the country or in all fields of religion, philosophy, art, knowledge, and science, they gave total support and for them, we reason that their ancestors exploited the backward people here thousands of years ago.

So, as a matter of remorse, you will be put behind for service, loan or allotment of government accommodation. See, the simple thing is that a person's progeny cannot be punished for his crime. In the same manner, about 50 or 100 generations or hundreds and thousands of years back whoever did or did not do whatever who are we to fix and charge their children? And why shall we do so?

This is a common rule that everyone should get a hundred percent opportunity. But, here 80 to 90% of opportunities are snatched from talented people and most of the opportunities or vacancies are reserved for a caste or class special. Now, what the upper castes are supposed to do with these 10 to 20% opportunities? They will look for some other option. There are some examples here that those who could not get admission in medical/IIT or selected in scientific posts here due to reservation, went to America and worked there and were honoured with Nobel Prize there for the work done.

Parul: No, the reservation is just 49 percent and not 80 to 90 percent.

Dr. Samar: 49 percent is the direct one. And I will tell you how it reaches up to 80 to 90 percent. 10 percent of seats are reserved for EWS (Economical Weaker Section). After 59 (49+10) percent there is the remaining 41 percent. There are many states which have reserved 33 to 50 percent seats for women i.e., Bihar, Madhya Pradesh, and Chhattisgarh. So, out of 41 percent, 50 percent is reserved and only 20.5 percent is remaining. Out of this also, there are reservations for handicapped, ex-servicemen, sportsperson, and compassionate ground appointment, etc. Now, how many opportunities are there for a General person? Hardly 10 to 15 percent and you have reserved 80 to 90 percent opportunities or seats for those so-called people who cannot walk hand in hand with times. After these 90 percent (49 percent SC/ST/OBC + 10 percent EWS + women + especially abled + Ex-servicemen + sport quota + compassionate appointment) how many non-reserved seats are there? What is this natural justice? This is justice with whom and injustice with whom?

Is this the fault of the General/Upper caste that he was born there? Is it his fault that he and his ancestors tried to advance in the development race instead of lying behind? Is it his fault that he is a male? Is it his fault that he is not a handicap? Is it his fault that he was not born to a Dalit or backward person? Is it his fault that he is intelligent? Is it his fault that his father is laborious and has been working hard, day and night in a multinational company to be included in the high-income group in place of remaining in the low-income group?

Parul: No, it is not his fault.

Dr. Samar: Then why he is punished? Those who have fetched less or much less marks in his comparison and belong to other class and caste or backward and Dalit are getting high posts. They get married in elite families to nice girls. One who is many times more intelligent, smart, active, energetic and strong to them is roaming here and there. That also till the time he again comes in the low-income group, or becomes poor or becomes economically backward or his whole community becomes backward, so that government includes them in Dalit quota. Is there any possibility of normal progress in such a country?

Parul: Yes, it makes a bit of difference.

Dr. Samar: Not a bit of it makes a lot of difference. Tell me, is there any country in the world where 80 to 90 percent opportunities are earmarked for backwardness and even 10 to 20 percent opportunities are not left for progressing ones. And the irony is that these 80 to 90 percent reservation people can also come in these 10 to 20 percent opportunities. Many times it happens that these opportunities are also provided to the reserved quota for various reasons. There is no country in the world with such a system. Now, tell me honestly people will opt for the progressive crowd or backward crowd? Which one is more beneficial to them? Why will they develop? And if people do not develop, then why and how will the nation develop?

If we want to develop and become an advanced and dynamic country, this discriminative reservation system shall come to end. Everyone must be provided with equal opportunities. Yes if it seems that there is some backwardness or illiteracy in some class, caste or family at any level, in reality, some other measures can be taken. This backwardness is much more in some castes and classes, for example, some people from SC or ST of some areas. For this, their level of education and economy has to be improved and they must be enthused and made aware of development and growth. Just remaining backward and undeveloped and taking advantage of the reservation as a parasite is not the solution to this problem. You can arrange for additional studies our coaching for them in the education system. Who knows, what happened thousands of years ago and it is not right, logical, appropriate and okay to punish their progeny for that.

Parul: Yes, the problem is there. Let us see, what can be done for it. Also, what is the better option available?

Dr. Samar: Many thanks for the assurance madam.

Parul: It was really nice meeting you. What else can I do for you?

Dr. Samar: You are invited to our school foundation day program next month. (Handing her the invite) If you come, we will be grateful and our students will take inspiration from you.

Parul: Certainly I will come. (After getting invitation she checked her diary and calendar she assures her availability and gets it noted.)

Time passes quickly. Loksabha's tenure is about to end. Preparation for the next elections has begun at a slow pace. Election code of conduct has been implemented. As the party had lost the last elections very badly, so they have changed the strategy now. Parul is the first among the star campaigners of the party. Elections begin with her as the star campaigner. Now, Parul knows how to use small or big, positive or negative things of the opposition well and she does it for her benefit.

Time flies, with it Parul has a strong grip on her party as well as the politics of the country. Now, she does not need to campaign much in her constituency as her name is a brand in itself and she can win from any constituency in India if she stands from there.

In politics, nationalism or benevolence to the country is a subject that can be made an issue at any time. It can be highlighted and the benefits can be reaped. Nationalism is a seed that is ready and gives fruit at the time when the user leader decides so. There are many leaders in the world who become nation heads by reaping the crop of nationalism. Parul does not want to lag behind and raises the issue assertively.

Seven

The time passes at a fast pace. Dorothy and George meet the other week. Dorothy relates all the problems in the field of research that developing countries have to face. George is surprised to know all this. Gradually, the meeting between George and Dorothy keeps growing and they become good friends, which in turn leads to them loving each other.

George and Dorothy complete their Masters and Ph.D. almost together. George starts teaching at a university. Dorothy is connected to UNEP (United Nations Environment Programme) and is posted at the regional office of UNEP in North America. Both decide to marry each other. Their marriage ceremony is held lavishly in the most famous church in her home state in India.

Soon, they go back to the USA from India. In the USA a formal home party is thrown upon. Both of them are working diligently and honestly in their respective fields. Dorothy starts working with the ecosystem division of the UNEP but, very soon she is attached to its communication division. The executive director of UNEP, Mr. David realises Dorothy's talent and devotion very early and gives her an important portfolio. While working at UNEP, Dorothy gives many innovative ideas. She works for making technology more affordable for developing countries. She relates disasters to climate change and exhibits how climate change has led to an increase in drought, flood, tsunami, etc., in a scientific manner.

Dorothy meets a colleague named Tony at UNEP. Tony is on the verge of retirement. Dorothy asks him about his work experiences at UNEP. He tells her about his limits there and as he is due for retirement now, he asks her to do all those things that may lead to the well-being of her, UNEP and the world.

Dorothy: What is the work that you could not do and that will lead to the welfare of everyone?

Tony: See, the biggest problem of the environment today is economic development leading to the spread of garbage and pollution. If you could give the right condition and direction to both, this will be for the welfare of all.

Dorothy: What can be done and how?

Tony: You have to think of better techniques for garbage disposal and also how to implement them on a local, regional, continental or global level? While working with UNEP, you will find how some specific techniques are being used in some places. It can work much better with slight changes as required at the global level.

Dorothy interacts with Tony on various topics and gets to know about his experience, reasons behind his success or failure in certain fields according to his expectations.

It is not that garbage management is a big problem in the developing and backward countries only, it is a hazard for some developed countries as well. Dorothy prepares an excellent model of garbage management for these countries. But, her most important work is to create awareness among locals regarding it.

During her job at UNEP, Dorothy visits Prayagraj (India) while the Kumbh fair is going on. She visits Kumbh out of curiosity, as this is the only place in the world where maximum people have gathered at a particular time. She wants to study from the environmental viewpoint the arrangement and influence of a huge crowd of billions of people near a river and that also for more than one month. This the reason behind her visit to Prayagraj during the Kumbh fair.

Dorothy makes a study of the Kumbh as per her point of view. She is surprised to find that the water of the river Ganga which was much polluted, suddenly becomes pollution-free and clean for one month. She reaches the conclusion that along with other small reasons, the main reason is the stoppage of the flow of sewage water in the river for a few months. Billions of devotees take bath in Ganga every day for more than one month and still the water remains clear and immaculate.

After this Kumbh visit, Dorothy reaches to the conclusion to do something for proper waste management. If solid and liquid waste could be managed properly and proper plantation is done, then the problem of water, land and air pollution may be solved altogether. She presents some solutions on the basis of her knowledge through a variety of experiences, which is already implemented in different places. She just popularizes it and implements it in other fields as well.

First of all, during her work Dorothy finds that other institutes of UNO like UNDP, FAO, UNESCO can be complementary to one another and if they work in unison on some particular issue, they can produce better results. Therefore, she establishes better coordination among UNDP, FAO, and UNESCO.

Dorothy makes proper arrangements to collect the waste from the fish market and non-veg market which was a big problem to urban bodies and led to the spread of bad odour, mess, and diseases. She sends it to duck farming stations where ducks eat it very happily. Through this, not only the mess is cleared but also the ducks start laying 24 eggs monthly in place of 8 to 10 eggs due to this waste from the fish market and non-veg market. Thus, the odorous and disease spreading mess of the fish and of the non-veg market turns into beautiful eggs of the duck on a grand scale.

Similarly, she helps to make better use of the routine garbage coming out from homes. She arranges to segregate the vegetable peels and other eatables. She segregates the rotten ones from those which are in good condition. She provides the vegetable peels and good eatables to the cattle which are unable to give milk or reproduce and roam about on roads. These cattle can give at least dung and now the amount of garbage in the form of dung has also lessened to one fourth.

Now, their dung is collected at a different place and methane gas is produced out of it, then that dung is fed to the earthworm. They, in turn, make the excellent quality of wormy cast manure which is also called black gold. This helps increase the fertility of the land and leads to sufficient growth in agricultural products and organic farming in the country. It means the waste is converted into excellent fertilizer in just 72 hours and that also without the use of electricity. It takes a minimum of 45 days to make fertilizer through the bacterial method and here it is ready in only 72 hours.

Similarly, rotten waste cannot be fed to the cattle, so it is separated and kept to produce maggots. These maggots grow by leaps and bounds and when a sufficient quantity of maggots are there, hens are brought there. They eat these maggots and produce nice eggs the next morning. There is nothing in the world that cannot make big eggs from waste and maggots.

There are many non-biodegradable items in this waste, mainly in plastic, that can be recycled and used again. If it is not used properly, mounds of waste or garbage are created. Even in the developed European continent, there are many islands that are filled with plastic.

She gives suggestions for better use of recyclable garbage. She popularizes the methods of making a specific Polymers like PP polypropylene, LDPE low-density polyethylene and HDPE high-density polyethylene from recyclable plastic container, bucket, chair, table, etc. which in turn can be converted into useful products i.e., anti-static, anti-microbial and anti-bacterial tiles. These tiles are very strong and cost-effective as well.

She also popularizes the other techniques of making many items from the recyclable plastic and dissolving non-biodegradable items by burning in such a way that no smoke comes out and therefore, it will be pollution-free. Their remains are used to fill the base of high rise buildings in place of soil and also for filling big ditches or in road construction.

Similarly, Dorothy also finds a suitable solution for liquid waste and popularizes the technique to treat dirty sewage water at a low cost to use it for irrigation. It does not flow into the main river, a separate pipeline has been arranged for it. This pipeline either runs with the river or is underground, so space is also saved.

Thus, sufficient water becomes available for irrigation which in turn increases the production of the country. Now, farmers do not have to depend on rainwater and agriculture is not a gamble with monsoon but a definite source of income.

During the summers, the rivers dry up but the pipelines supply the water of sewage treatment for irrigation and they never dry up. It has many benefits. The clean water of the river does not get polluted due to the flowing of sewage water into it. The farmers get regular water supply which is more fertile. It leads to sufficient growth in agriculture production. This pipeline is very cost-effective as it is made from recycled plastic and as it is laid adjacent to the river, it also saves space.

Dorothy finds that in backward countries, maximum homes have no toilet. They defecate in open which leads to the spread of diseases in two ways. The first one is through flies etc. from outside and secondly, since women had to wait for long till dark in the night, it causes diseases inside the body. Dorothy devises a model of cheap toilet which has two small pits. When one pit is filled, the other is used and when the other pit is also filled, till then the first one has converted into manure, which is used in farms. This goes on and on, i.e., the problem of the toilet gets solved very easily and cost-effectively.

Due to the awareness created by Dorothy, the disease brought deaths of children and others from dengue, chikungunya, malaria, etc. becomes slow, as these are caused by mosquitoes born in the garbage, the water collected in old tyres, or earthen pots, etc. in the residential area. Bacteria borne diseases like T. B., Cholera, plague, typhoid, diphtheria, etc. and other diseases are also controlled in great measure.

The dry or wet garbage that spread odour, filth, mental disturbance, and diseases yesterday, today due to efforts of Dorothy has been put to right use and thus has spread happiness, greenery, and light from the energy of biomass.

Dorothy's efforts result in the increase of average life expectancy in the countries with the lowest life expectancy like Chad, Guinea Bissau, Afghanistan, Swaziland, and Namibia, etc. from 50 - 52 years to 60-62 years. Likewise, in the countries with an average life expectancy of 60-62 years, it rises up to 68-70 years. Thus, the proper disposal of garbage and the use of the right technique has not only lowered the diseases but also helped increase the production of the country. The dark homes have now started sparkling with light and children are studying in it.

After proper waste disposal and increased life expectancy, Dorothy focuses on barren, waste, unproductive and deserted land to improve people's lives along with the environment. Dorothy thinks that if all the barren and wasteland of the world could be put to better use by means of some genetic changes and plants and flowers could be grown there, this will not only make earth green but may also help grow the income of local people. She makes available the medicinal, aromatic, edible and other plants that are grown by the research institute of America, Israel, China, India, and other major countries on a single platform.

In the biennial meeting of the UNEP governing body United Nations environment assembly, Dorothy submits a plan for proper use of barren, waste and unproductive land before all members of 193 countries.

Then, she plans her tours in various countries to meet the nation heads, local leaders and if needed to farmers also and educate them of the suitable plants for that place and motivates them. She has made it a campaign now. Only educated people knew UNEP to date, but now, those who could not keep pace with development, poor and farmers also know about it as it has made ample positive changes in their lives due to activism and dynamism.

Dorothy brings a change to the previous work culture. In place of organising meetings with some top officials or beaurocrats in 5 or 7-star hotels (who very soon get transferred to other departments or retire), she prefers to meet or communicate with the farmers or fishermen who are directly connected with those issues. She makes them aware of various aspects, profit, loss, etc. and motivates them through all her means and ways. She educates them about various plants to be planted in a particular area and climate that suit most to the economy and ecology. For example, eucalyptus is not good for countries like India as it absorbs more water and during summers it lacks water. So, Neem, Peepal or banyan are more useful for India and she suggests this to the government. Similarly, in other countries, she suggests for proper crops or plants to be grown in barren or wasteland area.

There are many varieties of crops that are already available in those countries and with some genetic or other changes, they become more suitable to the requirements of that area, climate, height, slope, rain, drought, and the land of alkalinity, etc. Dorothy gives solid solutions to the unproductive land, mountains, deserts, marsh, etc. for their proper use.

Consequently, the marshy land that used to be a source of rot and diseases, now has medicinal and aromatic plants like Brahmi (Bacopa monnieri), Gotu Kola (Centella asiatica) and sweet flag root (across calamus) flourishing with fragrance. This process involves aroma in place of rot, safety from diseases, eco-friendliness and also growth in the economy of the people of the area and country. This change can be felt in the happiness and tranquillity on the faces of inhabitants of the area.

The hilly area which signified scarcity, distress, poverty and desolation with stones all around, is now filled with shooting fragrance of lavender, sugar-free sweetness of stevia, greenery of geranium and buds of rosemary. Now, the inhabitants of those places are happy due to the commercial production of these plants. Agarwood oil is sold at rupees 15 lacs per litre and their faces are blooming like Rosemary Buds. The sweetness of stevia can be felt naturally in their behaviour.

The land devoid of irrigation and totally dependent on rains is now giving a new life and direction to the nation by producing Palmaroja, Sena (casia anestophylis), Withaniya, Ocimum, Lemongrass, etc.

The areas with a bit of irrigation system are producing basil, peppermint, menthol, mint, citronella, chamomilla, isabgol, rose, etc. They are contributing to the economy of the country in an important manner by alleviating the imbalance in the balance of payment accounts.

The villages were situated on the river banks, their people evacuated due to erosion every year and the land also become unproductive loamy soil earlier. Now, due to plantation of Khus (Vetiver), the erosion has stopped, and it is also helping in employment and increased income of the people as its roots produce oil and stem other handcrafted items. So, the rivers that were bane for the area, now they have become boon.

The areas with landslide have early growth of bamboo trees and it works as a wall there. Now, it has become the base of the lives of the inhabitants there as it has become an excellent source of income. Furniture and other useful items are made from it.

The land which was unable to produce anything due to acidity, now it is producing asparagus, patchouli, ginger, and spices to add to the taste of the meal. The desert area which looked dreary and desolate with sand only now looks green and fragrant with vetiver, asparagus, and white pestle plants.

Similarly, Dorothy brings the individual or collective efforts of people for environment protection to fore at world platform and motivates other societies and countries for sustainable development which will upgrade the future of their generations in turn. Lack of resources does not matter much, only strong willpower, dedication, and rendering to the environment conservation matters. This is what Dorothy puts as an example before the world.

She gives an example of Jadhav Pieng, a tribal from Assam, whose economic condition is not well, grows a forest on 1350 acres of barren land without any government aid. Now, there is no land erosion, no sand layers on productive land or no sand-filled storm during the summer as Brahmaputra river is visible there. Brahmaputra River which was considered to be the curse of Assam has now emerged as a boon for farmers, tribal and villagers because of the efforts of a single person. If everyone in the society makes efforts on the individual level or collectively, all the environment-related issues will disappear and earth will be enriched with pure water, forest, fertile land, and animals.

Dorothy gets promoted as deputy executive director in UNEP and works for better coordination between various regional offices so that eco-friendly products of one area get publicized and implemented in the other regions as well. She establishes better coordination and proper communication among six regional offices in various continents and the headquarters at Nairobi. It means an eco-friendly product in Asia is also advertised and people are made aware of it in Asia Pacific, Africa, Latin America, etc. regional offices. She also establishes better harmony among other related institutes, such as UNDP UNESCO and FAO.

UNEP gets better scientific and technical aid from UNDP, UNESCO, and FAO. All four institutes provide science and technique related updated information and facilities in various fields like environment conservation, poverty alleviation, food preservation, and climate change. People's culture is associated with environmental conservation and science now. The plantation and water conservation done traditionally in some areas has obtained an organised scientific aspect now. UNEP is playing an important role in providing the best varieties of seeds, manure and techniques as per the region's environment and ecosystems and helping positively those countries and their farmers to import less and export more. All these events may be attributed to Dorothy's help.

Any better technique available in any region of the world is changed and modified accordingly for other countries by Dorothy and the political leadership of the concerned country is informed about it. This much useful technique brings drastic changes in most of the countries and proves to be an ideal sample of the works and efforts taken for all humanity.

Cost-effective smog towers are constructed in many cities of different countries in the world where the air has been polluted very much, too clean billions of cubic metre of air every day. The enzyme that rots plastic is made cheaper and easily available, so that plastic decays in a few days and can be recycled. Houses built near forests would easily catch fire from forest fires which led to death and destruction. Today the technique of building fire-resistant houses is available to everyone which helps to save lives and belongings.

In flood-hit areas, each year lakhs of people were adversely affected by the flood, but now floating homes can be built easily by cheap and conveniently available material. In the deserts, fog collectors are made available which converts fog into the water for drinking and farming and water reaches all homes through pipelines. Transparent solar windows are made which help in producing electricity from sunlight economically when installed in houses. These windows make electricity by absorbing infrared light. All these techniques save people from pollution and provide ease and economic strength to the lives of mankind in general.

While working with UNEP, Dorothy meets one Abraham who lives a much luxurious life. Although no one is bothered with his luxurious lifestyle, the objection is on his thought and viewpoint to the environment. Even a common educated man cares for small things like the use of heater or AC when needed, opening water tap only if required, not leaving the vehicle on unnecessarily and properly disposing of trash, etc. But Abraham does not care for all these.

Coincidentally Dorothy and Abraham had a detailed talk on the issue of the environment.

Dorothy: It is the duty of each individual to help in conserving the environment. You should follow small rules for it.

Abraham: Nobody is born out of environmental conservation and neither any human can pollute or destroy it. The earth which has preserved mankind for centuries, humans need not think about that earth and its environmental conservation. The earth is capable of conserving its environment.

Dorothy: When humans lived as troglodytes, no artificial equipment or environment pollutant was a part of their lifestyle. At that time, the earth renewed and conserved its environment by itself. But now, the population is growing by leaps and bounds. Moreover, we are depleting the environment rapidly. It means if the earth is conserving and renewing its environment arithmetically and we are using its resources and polluting environment geometrically. This gap or difference between arithmetic and geometric has to be reconciled, only then our earth and its environment and resources may remain safe and conserved.

Abraham: I know that when the population was not much and the environment was not polluted, the environment was capable to renew itself. If you go back to the 17th or 18th century, the people then could not get a proper meal and even developed countries like England had an average life expectancy of 40-41 years only. But, as you say, now, we have polluted the environment to a large extent. Still, due to the green revolution, white revolution, etc. the production and supply of food and milk have grown immensely. On the other hand, despite the emission of chlorofluorocarbon from AC, fridge, etc. and carbon monoxide, carbon dioxide, lead, sulphur, nitrous oxide from vehicles and industries, the average life expectancy has gone up to 70 years or even above it. The average life expectancy in the eco-friendly era was almost half of this. So, I do not care about the environment and in fact, no one should doubt the earth's capacity to conserving its own ecosystem.

Dorothy: In the 17th - 18th-century life expectancy was low due to a high death rate, and it had nothing to do with environmental pollution or lack of it. In that period, better and advanced medical technologies and medicines were not available. And yes, if you pay attention to the environment in today's age of excellent medical techniques, the average life expectancy will go over 85 to 90 years from the present 72 years in the whole world. In the same way, some resources like water, coal, and petroleum are available in a limited measure, so we must focus on their optimal use and sustainable development otherwise this polluted development may swallow the earth and may cause havoc to us and our coming generations.

Abraham: See, in 17th -18th century's resources were used less and people had to face scarcity of basic amenities like bread, house, and clean water. In the present scenario, the resources are exploited to make new useful objects and life is becoming more comfortable. We should not worry about environmental pollution and exploitation of resources as we trust science and it will find some solution to it. At least some arrangements are made for settlement on the Moon and Mars or new and renewable energy sources have been discovered before the petroleum reserves exhaust. This will follow in every sphere.

Dorothy: Do you know how difficult and costly it could be to settle on the Moon or Mars? It will take many generations to shift from here and settle there. If we pay little attention to the earth and keep the environment clean, this will become very beautiful and liveable as if the hypothesis of heaven on earth may come true.

Abraham: See, whatever you have read or understood, you are speaking according to it. I have great respect for your ideas but my thoughts are different regarding this, actually very different.

Dorothy: What do you mean by different?

Abraham: You are worried about these petty issues. You should not work so hard on it separately. It should be inculcated in the school curriculum of children so that they will become aware of all these things very early and environmental conservation will be a part of their routine and culture. Yes, it may be that there are a few exceptions like me, but that will not make much difference. If you really wish to do something for the environment, then do it on a large scale? I am an extremist and speak like that. If you do something from your level, you will certainly succeed in saving the earth and its ecosystem.

Dorothy: Now please tell what needs to be done on which grand scale?

Abraham: See, there are a number of coal mines in the world that are ablaze in the land and the coal is burning to ashes and destroyed. This is also harming the environment along with the destruction of the resources itself. You should focus on developing the technique to extinguish this fire.

Dorothy: Great idea! What else can we do?

Abraham: Every year billions of hectares of forests are charred on the earth. How many days it took to control the fire in the forests of Amazon, you saw. This is truly destructive for all living beings, plants and the environment. Try to develop a technique that informs the region, country or UNEP is connected to the satellite the moment it catches fire in the forest and the fire is controlled immediately by extinguishing it. The low-cost artificial rain by silver iodide, anti-fire liquid or wax or any other advanced technique must be developed to control the fire. We all know that fire needs three things; fire, burning substance and oxygen. If one of these three is removed, the fire will blow out automatically. So, try to invent the technique to segregate oxygen, trees or fire from huge forest fires so that it extinguishes easily.

Dorothy: Oh my God! You are a great environmental thinker. What else can be done to save the earth and ecosystem?

Abraham: I know that you have worked a great deal for barren, vacant and unproductive land of the earth. Still, a huge segment of the earth is lying vacant, barren, unproductive and unused especially in mountains and deserts. This unproductive land and desert are expanding per annum. If suitable and eco-friendly trees are planted here to stop this desertification and expansion of the barren land, nothing can be better than it.

Dorothy: I am more than glad to meet you. It was my good luck that I could meet you.

Abraham (interrupting her): Yes and if you really wish to focus on petty issues then do it in the villages or backward areas of cities where subsidised or supplied for a monthly charge, electricity is misused on a large scale. No one there bothers to switch off the bulb or electricity even during the day time. Water taps keep leaking and lots of water is wasted. If the government or any other institute gives subsidy on taps and flushes like it was done for LED bulbs, maximum work can be done in optimum use of water and its conservation. 5 to 7 litres of water is wasted through tap and flush during a single toilet use in the traditional toilet. You can see the use of 20 years old diesel vehicles in villages even today, although diesel vehicles are prohibited from use after ten years. I think it will be better for the environment if these small measures are taken care of.

Dorothy: Really, I am so impressed after meeting you. Thanks for your great ideas and I will try to do something better in these directions for sure. Thanks again.

They take leave. Dorothy is now aware of Abraham's environment-friendly ideas also which may add to her future endeavors.

The annual COP (Conference of the Parties) at the United Nations climate change conference is being held. But it is not very successful due to the lack of commitment by some major greenhouse emitting nations. Dorothy is disappointed and disheartened but she is not ready to cede. She decides to visit all the countries which are backing off from the commitment to greenhouse gas and carbon emission and meet and speak to their top leadership on various levels. She will not only make them implement the commitment of the last COP but will motivate them to the core. Dorothy travels to many countries in this order.

While working with UNEP, Dorothy gradually visits many countries in the world and their top leaderships, to solve their misconceptions of economic issues related to climate change. She informs them that there are more benefits to be harnessed in comparison to the expenses on the issues of global warming and climate change.

She knows well that the final decision will be taken by the top leadership but if the top bureaucrats, public and opposition parties agree and unite for the cause, the leadership will have no other option but to follow COP and save the earth. She acts tactfully. She first of all talks to the advisors and bureaucrats of the top leaders of the countries who are reluctant to implement the decisions of the COP. She convinces them and also explains the effects of climate change to the media and opposition leaders through detailed statistical charts. Media also co-operates with Dorothy on these issues. At last, the top leaderships are also convinced and agree to it. She uses different logic for different top leaders of the countries.

She tells the leaders of the countries that have large coastal areas that if the temperature goes up by 2 degrees Celsius in comparison to the industrial revolution, many of your islands and coastal areas will submerge into the ocean. If you compare the cost of the submerged lives, areas and resources to the expenses that might be incurring on implementation of the decision of COP, Paris Treaty or providing a healthy environment to the citizens of your beautiful country with natural islands and coasts, the former will be much more.

She gives the example of the Krakatau mountain of Indonesia to some heads of nations as to how it was 340 meters high in August 2008 and after a tsunami caused by the volcanic eruption in December 2008, it is now one-third of its original height, i.e., 110 meters only. If the snow on the glaciers melts rapidly due to global warming, the sea level will rise and destructive tsunamis will become a danger to not only small islands but large countries as well.

She tries to convince the leaders of the countries which are not situated near the sea and explains how expenses are incurred on cancer, skin diseases, respiratory and lung-related diseases along with the psychological and humanitarian sufferings of the relatives and acquaintances of the patients. If we try to count it on the basis of the economy, it will be dishonest to compare health or peace to some dollars. Still, if we do so, it will be better to save the earth.

Thus, you can see that you have to spend much less on COP and implementing the Paris Treaty in comparison to the health and happiness of the people of your country.

Dorothy tries to logically convince the developed countries that you know the exercise for setting on the various other planets is carried on at a fast pace. But if only 0.000001 percent of the cost of these exercises is spent on the earth and its environment, the earth and your country will have an abundance of greenery and happiness and it will be eco-friendly in the real sense of the term.

Gradually, Dorothy's efforts start showing and all the major countries of the world including America agree to it. Again a conference is held on climate change and all the countries agree to the conditions of climate change.

Dorothy and George are on a personal visit to India during the summer. When her friend and neighbour Alice comes to know of her stay, she comes to meet them accompanied by her husband Peter. All four are doing chit chat which gradually focuses on the most featured issue of water, that how the Government of India is sending water to Vidarbha and other areas of the country by train for easy living. Dorothy is surprised to see the condition of some regions as the country which is devastated every year because of flood, many fights, murders, and suicides are caused for "water" and nothing else in summers.

In the meantime, Dorothy's mothers' puts four glasses of water on the table for them. Then, tea, snacks, etc. are served.

Peter (sipping tea): See, here everyone talks and worries about improvement but nobody wants to do it on one's own level.

Dorothy: Means?

Peter: Four glasses of water are here. Somebody takes one or two sips and throws the rest of the water in drains.

Alice: So, how does this meagre amount of water matter?

Peter: This wastage of four glasses of water you have seen here. But, this is the same in almost all homes in India. If a guest comes, he is served water first. India's population is 130 crores. If only 5 crores of homes are visited by guests and four glasses of water are drained away in every home, it means crores of liters of water are wasted daily in the name of guests.

George: It has broader macro effects.

Peter: Just now you saw only wastage of water in glasses but more water is wasted.

Dorothy: But how?

Peter: See this is RO water which flows down many glasses of water to purify these four glasses of water. Then the water will be wasted again to wash those served glasses. George, suppose a gentleman does not like to waste the water and sips the full glass. So he will go to the urinal and use the flush, again wastage of the water. You can see this the culture of the side effect of this small water tradition to welcome the guest.

Alice: Let us change and improvise this culture from today itself. We will keep a bottle of water and glass in place of serving water in glasses. If they wish they will drink water, it will not be wasted then.

Dorothy: We have to save water and create awareness among people on national as well as international levels. Any culture or system that destroys water or other natural resources must be changed immediately.

George: Which are the other places where water is wasted?

Peter: Like many people keep the water tap on while shaving or brushing their teeth. If the tap is leaking, they take two-three days to get it repaired. In the same way, the shower is kept open for long during bathing. So much water is wasted by all these, leave aside the village and farms.

George: Plants are not irrigated here through sprinkler irrigation? Is there some other method of irrigation in practice?

Peter: Maximum irrigation is done here through the traditional method. Only 5% or even less is done by sprinkler irrigation.

George: What are the measures taken for water harvesting here?

Peter: Recently, people have become aware, otherwise, most of the rainwater is still wasted.

Dorothy: Now there is a water crisis and just two months there will be the problem of excess water and floods because of rain. The government must form a solid policy to balance the flood and drought situations. This will let people understanding the value of water and pay attention to every drop, thus more crop on one hand and let them learn better water harvesting techniques on others. This may end the water crisis in India or any other country in the world.

Alice: The value of water must be taught to each and every citizen of the country. Water is life, life begins with water and it will be comfortable only till the water lasts.

Peter: So, we talked so much and now it is time to leave. Do visit us if you find some time.

Peter and Alice take leave from them and Dorothy decides to focus mainly on eradicating water scarcity and ensure clean potable water to drink as well as irrigation and other uses on the global level. She becomes more sensitive to the issue when during various levels of talks, she is made to listen to the sentence that the next world war may commence for water.

Meanwhile, during her study about the availability of water, Dorothy finds that 97% of the available water on earth is in the seas which is brine and not usable at all. 1.5% of water is on poles and glaciers in the form of snow, which is far from the reach of common people. Only 1% approximately is available as rivers, lakes, underground water, etc., on which mankind depends.

To make available clean water is not only necessary for the present generation but also to ensure the continuous supply of water to the coming generations. Dorothy meets the people connected to water conservation works and comes to know about their techniques, processes, and activities. Then, she also educates herself on the available latest techniques in the field of water conservation.

She takes the help of all her 6 regional offices, meetings of UNEP governing body and other mediums to create awareness about the various prevalent water conservation techniques in the other parts of the world to ensure clean and availability of water.

The best available technique to convert heavy water into soft water, she finds in Israel. She encourages rainwater harvesting and recharging underground water on different regional levels through available better techniques. She tries to popularize specific taps and flushes which ensure maximum work done through minimum water consumption.

When they complain about the lack of resources, she gives the example of Javang Nafel, a farmer's son who created 15 artificial glaciers on his own in Ladakh without any government aid. He found that there is plenty of water and snow during winters but during summers they had to face scarcity of water. So, he slowed down and diverted the main stream flowing from the mountains in winter and collected the water in small dams which got frozen. It was used for drinking and farming during summer.

While working as the deputy executive director of the UNEP, Dorothy requests the governments of different countries to connect the rivers as far as possible which solves both the problems of flood and drought. Now, the rainwater that flows into rivers, is put to the best possible use.

Just like the year 2013 was declared as the international year of water co-operation, this year was declared the International year of optimum water utilisation.

More and more plantation is done to attract rains. All these coordinated efforts solve the problem of water from the earth to a great extent and the earth looks lush green, clean and satiated.

Similarly, Dorothy helps to reach the benefits of new eco-friendly researches to all the countries, regions, farmers and to all who need it. The focus is on new and renewable energy at less cost in providing better technology and easy access. For example, in the countries situated adjacent to the equator, the tropic of cancer and the tropic of capricorn where plenty of sunlight comes, she constructs solar windows with a transparent frame which create energy from infrared rays. She puts stress on the technique and use of wind energy in deserts and the use of tidal energy in coastal areas. Use of new and renewable energy in place of non-renewable energy frees the environment from pollution and since the import of petroleum comes down, the countries payment imbalance is also balanced. Many countries that imported petroleum products and energy, now have converted into exporters of the same.

Consequently, the expenditure on global warming and climate change by various countries not only gives environmental benefits but also economic benefits many times more. A decline in the import of petroleum products, increase in the production of cheap renewable energy, enhanced groundwater level, clean river water, breathable air, increased production of fruits, flowers, wood, shellac, silk, etc. lead to the increase of people's income in different countries. With environmental improvement in the level of income, health and life expectancy also follow it.

Dorothy's efforts flower and flourish and people need not worry about Global warming and climate change as there is a lot of awareness now. It was noticed that in the beginning the goal of bringing down the increasing temperature was fixed to less than 2-degree celsius and now it is about 1.5-degree celsius. In the last COP, the member countries have gone ahead from the commitments in the Paris Treaty. Some new problems have also been solved. All these are possible due to Dorothy's unforgettable contribution.

Eight

Geeta and Gurmeet head to the nearest police station. There they get to know that a new police officer has joined, by the name of Khushwant Singh Gill.

They want to instantly meet him. Females seldom arrive at the station and this leads to a quick meeting with the officer. Now coincidently, Gurmeet realises that the officer is his childhood friend. Khushwant Singh offers them tea and snacks and enquires about Gurmeet's well-being. However, Gurmeet wants to discuss the matter at hand first so she urges him to listen and hands over the recording to him.

Khushwant Singh becomes serious and discusses this with his senior officers. After some time he asks Geeta and Gurmeet to go home and that they will be contacted if further help is needed. And so they must keep their mobile phones nearby. Now, it is up to the security agencies. If Moinuddin calls, they must behave as if nothing has occurred although it is not likely he will call.

Not only in India, but it is also the case with the police forces all over the world that they could not act on time. The other side of this coin is that if when we needed, the police forces coordinate with the security agencies to reach a particular goal.

Only Munna's phone number is available, but it is switched off and the last location shows near Gurmeet's home. However, the car number plates have been recorded on the CCTV. Also, the place and location of various attacks are now known through the recording.

The Prime Minister's roadshow is at 4 o'clock in the evening so whatever needs to be done it has been done within these 3 to 4 hours only.

Meanwhile, Moinuddin's flight lands at the Srinagar airport and he switches his mobile back from flight mode and becomes aware of the updates. His mobile with a special SIM card has only a few stored numbers of special terrorists. He talks to them one by one and ensures things are in the right order. After this, he moves towards the main city of Srinagar via a taxi cab. From Srinagar, he takes a mini truck towards Muzaffarabad. He is happy inside as his plans are about to come to fruition. These events would cause a great deal of damage to India economically, socially, politically and culturally. His bounty would increase.

A man's happiness more than doubles when not only he achieves his mortal desires but has also achieved his goals for the afterlife. Munna is happy that he got two birds with one shot. On one hand, he will receive a healthy sum of money for his work and on the other, there will be huge devastation in India, a rival country. India would recede on the world map and the cause of making Dar-ul- Harb (Non-Islamic Nation) to Dar- ul- Islam (Islamic Nation) would get a huge boost.

He would get 72 virgins in heaven and 80 thousand kafir servants will be there. Moinuddin feels that his contributions to the cause would get him personal prosperity. His imaginations are running wild. He thinks that not only ISIS but other jihadi groups would also reward him handsomely.

He thinks that on the day of judgment, akhirat, his dead body would spring back to life. He will be the first among many thousands of Muslims to reach heaven. There will be no problems and only happiness and prosperity waiting for him in the afterlife. When people of lesser mental capacity see that they have enough money for a lifetime, their ego knows no bounds. Munna feels that the more kafirs he kills, a more religious man he would be considered. He would get virgins in this life as well as the afterlife.

Generally, every religion believes in tit for tat. Science states that for every action, there is an equal and opposite reaction. When a man dies, with him die several memories and relationships. When after committing such countless murders, a man thinks he will go to heaven, it shows his immaturity, mean mindedness and foolishness and also of the people who propagate religion in such a way.

His immature brain could have gotten some semblance of contentment for a short while but he had a long time of pain and hurt waiting on him. The security agencies had his number.

The security agencies were working on two levels. They sounded red alert, and the security was tightened for the four cities to be targeted and the five places marked by the terrorists. Along with that, the plan was being carried out to eliminate the terrorists lodged in hotels or outside.

Two vehicles equipped with sirens and red-blue flashing lights were intercepted in Varanasi. It was not possible to apprehend them in their hotels so the firefight began outside. Ten of the terrorists are shot dead, none is caught alive.

Their mobile phones are found and would come handy. The numbers of the terrorist who were in Chandigarh, Ahmedabad, and Mumbai is found along with Moinuddin personal number. Some other numbers of terrorist-like Dr. Shuaib and Professor Gilani are found on the phone. Born and bred on this land but helping the terrorists. Now, the terrorists in Mumbai are shot dead with the help of the information found on the phone. Rahman, waiting to assassinate the Prime Minister during roadshow was also apprehended. The operatives in Chandigarh came to known of these developments.

The terrorists in Chandigarh, leave their cars behind and hijack a school bus, changing their target from airport to Punjab Legislative

Assembly. They hatch a plan to make the MLAs hostage. As they are proceeding with this, a firefight ensues with the security agencies. Shots are fired from both sides. Grenades are deployed and four terrorists are killed. Eight security personnel were martyred. Six of the terrorists are about to enter the Legislative Assembly premises but suddenly a CISF Sub Inspector, risks his life, killing all of them and giving his life.

Moinuddin, in his truck heading towards Muzaffarabad, dreams of Victory. His phone rings and he is informed about the ongoing. He learns about the developments and he felt the ground slipping under his feet.

Before he could respond, his truck was stopped, and he is easily captured. Just now he was daydreaming of heaven and suddenly his life becomes worse than hell.

He is brought to Delhi and is incarcerated. Criminal cases in India usually take longer to process, so now in the gallows he dreams of hanging rope in place of virgins.

There comes a time in a man's life that things occur opposite to their expectations, emotions, and desires. Even the gold turns to the soil when he puts his hand on it. In such times, a man questions his existence, his belief in God. Cynicism takes over. A man who is optimistic and patient in such an hour has the potential to reach the epitome of greatness. A cool person under pressure turns to diamond. Our problems are nothing when we realise the odds that people like Jesus Christ, Prophet Muhammad, Lord Ram, Gautama Buddha, Mahaveer, and Krishna had against them.

A movie director assigns the most difficult role to someone he knows has the capability to do justice to. Gurmeet is going through a rough patch in her life. She is unable to come to terms with the fact the person who was assisting her in social development, who would talk of world development all the time would come out like a demon who preyed on innocent lives. She could not believe she chose such a person, such an evildoer as her life partner.

When the night falls Geeta urges a shell shocked Gurmeet to stay with her for the night. Gurmeet refuses however she gives in when Geeta insists. She contemplates the whole night about the turn of events. Her only solace is that she played a vital role in foiling the plans of destroying her homeland.

The next day, Gurmeet's parents come to know about the development and proceed to their home. Gurmeet wants to leave Geeta's place but Geeta wants her to stay until her parents arrive. But Gurmeet, as courageous she is, readies herself citing pending work. She tells Geeta that she has taken enough of her precious time already and would now like to try to move on. To try and normalise her life.

When a person is happy and delighted, they love to share it with family and friends but in times of sadness, they choose to brood alone. Such is the nature of a typical human being.

Gurmeet has no shortage of people in her circle. She has burdened herself with growth and development be it kids, specially-abled or older citizens. All of them sympathize with her and wish to provide solace but she refuses to meet any of them, citing a case of headache.

Her parents, en route, are pondering about her well-being. They never really liked the Munna guy in any way. Why would their daughter decide to be with him was beyond them. They reach home in the evening. Gurmeet, who was lying on the bed, contemplating life, sprung on her legs and embraces her mother tightly.

Gurmeet is a strong-headed person but see melts in her mother's arms and begins to sulk. She would soon be asleep in her mother's lap. Her parents are her sanctuary.

She opens her eyes at midnight. Among all the despair, she sees hope. Hope that she saved the country, that she played a pivotal role in foiling terrorist plans.

Meanwhile, her old friend Khushwant Singh Gill, who is now a police officer in the area, tries and makes time for Gurmeet. It could be his interest in her cause, could be his care for depressed Gurmeet. He would discuss many topics with her. Sometimes agreeing, not so much at others. Like if there is God. Gurmeet believes that there is. That he/she saved her. Khushwant opines that scientist Stephen Hawkins says there is no such thing as God and the afterlife. And if there was God, why would things like murder and rape occur? Why would God not save innocent creatures from calamity? All these discussions would serve to bring them both closer. Human bonds formed in the toughest of time cure strongest.

In the meantime, Khushwant is transferred to nearby Gurugram from Faridabad. His parents want him to settle and get married. He does have feelings for Gurmeet but he is unable to confess them in her presence. All his courage vanishes when it comes to her. One day he jokingly asks her about her plans for marriage but she chooses to change the topic.

Khushwant's family asks him to marry a girl of his choosing, to which he replies to them to talk to Gurmeet's parents. Both their parents agree but Gurmeet has no expectations from the institution of marriage. She, however, gives in to her parents and Khuswant's wishes, or maybe it was her feelings for him.

Now there is an issue that she is not yet divorced from Munna. Usually, such matters take time to resolve but since Munna alias Moinuddin is a proclaimed terrorist, this was an open and shut case. Due to Khushwant's efforts, all the formalities are taken care of and the divorce is done. They both eventually get married and start leading a happy and content marriage life.

No matter how much the evil tries, it is the good side which eventually wins. Moinuddin keeps waiting for he is soon to be hanged. He lives in fear but eventually, the day comes and he is hanged, ending all the evil he had within himself.

Khushwant fulfills all his duties honestly while Gurmeet continues her great cause of social service. She would arrange books for the underprivileged children, would counsel unemployed youth, and arrange bicycles for the needy, helping people with loans and setting up senior citizen homes for the elderly. She would do all she could to help everyone.

In due time she realises that instead of treating the symptoms, she needs to cure the disease itself. She wants people to be self-sufficient and she would act as a catalyst. She first turns her direction of work from social services to social work. She starts paying attention to children as they are the future. She takes it upon herself to fight social evils like abortion, especially of the girl child's.

The law was already in place but nobody would enforce them. If she is successful in preaching women that how can a female let another female child die, it would be great. She would plead to their maternal instincts. She deploys her women followers for this task. She tells them that there is no difference between a girl child and a boy child. A girl can also work in space and military sectors. They can one day become great like Indira Gandhi, Indira Nui or Kalpana Chawla in their respective fields. Her efforts are fruitful and the sex ratio of the very region is improving.

She advocates education as a basic birthright for everyone. She wants every child born to get to school and she is playing a pivotal role in the cause. She finds people are unaware of getting their child vaccinated and so she does whatever is possible on a social, personal level to spread awareness about these issues. She would preach that children are not only a gift from God but are the future of the nation. She wants people to take pride in the fact that they send their child to school, get them inoculated and take time to further this great cause.

She has always been there to assist the unemployed and/or troubled youth. Helping them procure loans, do career counselling, helping them with start-ups. She wants to see their transformation from job seekers to job providers.

There always have been regulations in place for the care of the elderly but seldom are they deployed. After extensive research, she concludes that the parents do not wish to be a burden on their children. She senses that the people living in the old age homes have years of experience. However, they do have their own set of problems.

There are those who have retired from high paying posts, those parents of NRIs. They have their own set of beliefs. And those from the poor walk of life, the abandoned seniors, they lack confidence and seem to have an inferiority complex. As she identifies these two kinds, she shifts them into two different buildings. She wants these two groups to sportingly sort out their differences.

Once those who believe are learned and retired from high posts, they are tasked with giving lectures as visiting advisors in an educational or research institute. This will satisfy their egos while also earn money for senior homes. Similarly, she tasks others with teaching primary, middle or high school depending upon their skill. The other lesser fortunate seniors, she employs them in cottage industries like incense making.

She contacts bigger temples and organisations to collect dried flowers which would then be used to make incense sticks and rose water. All these efforts were coming together and would alleviate the burden from Gurmeet's shoulders. Not only financially but mentally. She gave them hope and a cause to live further. She instilled confidence and positive change in the people of old age homes.

When a person is self-motivated, they do not care much for courtesies laid down by society although the society does respect such persons. The Indian government would bestow Gurmeet with the Padma Shree award for all the unselfish acts she had done for the people and society.

She would go on to gain national recognition, various governmental and private institutes and organisations would invite her as their chief guest. As her name grows internationally, she would go on to receive the Ramon Magsaysay Award by the government of the Philippines. Eventually, the Indian government would award the Padma Vibhushan, the second-highest civilian honour.

If someone does not get an award for a job or act done towards the betterment of society and humankind, it simply means they were too busy doing their work. However if a person is awarded multiple times on an international level, it is sure that the person has given their best.

Gurmeet's unselfish acts have made her life more than significant. She has supported people from every walk of life, she has had so many blessings of these people. A person's life is complete when: 1 - He/she has sound health, 2 - Is financially sound enough to help others in need, 3 - Has a great relationship and chemistry with their spouse or partner, 4 - Has well learned and cultured children, and are capable, 5 - He/she is well known and has a high standing in society.

All of the above are seldom found across all the peoples of the world. It is either one of the two. Call it a coincidence that Gurmeet is amongst those rare specimens to have it all.

She is fit and healthy, making people happy gives her mental happiness. She is financially sound and has a loving husband in Gurmeet. She has meritorious children and is well known among international circles.

The same Gurmeet who had lost so much, who could not figure out her next move in life, who felt at the epitome of despair, was now a world-renowned example of a model human being. All clues to her hard work and perseverance.

One day, Gurmeet receives a phone call, she is pleasantly happy and surprised to hear the voice on the other side. It was her special friend Dorothy who is now the General Secretary of the United Nations. They would talk for hours. Dorothy would invite her to visit her New York home, along with her family. Dorothy tells Gurmeet that she will call Parul next. Parul will be at the UNO offices, representing India and so she will ask her to take a small detour to New York. It will be a great get-together, just like in college.

Gurmeet promises Dorothy that she will visit her in New York as she really wants to see her again. As far as family is concerned, that will depend upon husband and children's holidays. However, she will still try to get all of them together.

Nine

After elections, Parul's party forms the government and she gets a major portfolio in the cabinet. She becomes the finance minister. Although Parul had been a student of political science, after a certain level in life, experience works more than education.

Meanwhile, after the formation of the government, Transparency International issues the Corruption Perception Index (CPI), India has fallen from 75th to 82nd position. The issue becomes a hot topic of discussion in the country that in one year India has climbed seven steps of corruption. Parul is worried and calls the finance secretary to know the reasons and solutions. She wants to erase the monster named corruption from the country. The finance secretary enters the chamber.

Parul: Have you seen the position of India in the CPI issued by Transparency International? It has gone down seven points. We want to erase this monster named corruption from the country.

Finance Secretary: Yes madam, I saw it.

Parul: Just seeing is not enough. You have to find ways of ending corruption. What are the probabilities and how to do it? How many days it will take to do this pious job? Prepare a proper road map and do let me know.

Finance Secretary: Madam, there are two aspects of corruption. The first is theoretical, and the second is practical. Lack of education, awareness, low-income level, etc. are theoretical reasons. But if we see on the practical level, we find that the one who is most educated, like tax officer, IAS IPS, etc. or the one who is on highest post like chief engineer, ministers, etc. or the one who is most aware, like police officer, administrative officer, etc., is more prone to bribery and corruption.

Parul: In such a situation, what are the measures to counter corruption? How to solve this problem? Has it been controlled somewhere?

Finance Secretary: There is not much corruption in the central government except some departments like Income tax, Central Excise, Customs, CPWD, etc. Although there is much improvement even in these departments.

Parul: Then where do we find corruption mostly?

Finance Secretary: In state governments, like I enumerated a certain few departments in the central government where corruption ensues, there are only a few in the state government where there is no corruption. Even those departments were not easy to point out. The corruption in state government is outrageous! They seek bribe even to transport the dead body after the post-mortem to the crematorium. State department's like land, police, tax, transport, and narcotics, et al., the less is said about them the better.

Parul: Be it the central government or the state, I am talking about India overall. We need a solution to all the rampant corruption.

Finance Secretary: According to a consensus, 51% of people in India pay/take bribes. There was this specific Chief Minister who had tribal origins and was from a poor background. Coincidently he becomes a chief minister and got so involved in corruption and fraudulent practices that he ends up buying a diamond mine in Africa! In place of helping fellow people, coming from the same background as his, he kept all his ill earned riches for himself. The corruption has pervaded the mentality of people to such an extent that a government official earning a salary of 80000 to 90000 rupees per month seeks bribe from labour, rickshaw puller who's earning is meagre rupees 200 per day, for doing the job that the government has hired and posted them for in the first place. They do it without batting an eyelid.

Parul: The problem is as clear as the day. What needs to be done is to find a solution for it.

The finance secretary: We need to work on two levels for this. If we take the case of the central government, only some departments indulge in the practice of corruption. More transparency needs to be practiced, corruption prevention squads need to be deployed and modus operandi of the departments need to be more and more online and embracing technology. The service people and the officers need to be re-allocated the work repeatedly and even stricter punishments need to be introduced. The bigger the bribe sought, the harsher the punishment. The corruption could be curtailed to a big extent by the aforementioned practices. The meat of the issue, however, is state governments.

Parul: What sort of issues? If the state government is willing and the central government is helping, I don't see why we cannot get rid of this social evil.

Mr. Secretary: I am not stating that corruption cannot be weeded out. However, there are many hurdles. The main being that corruption has deeply pervaded their work culture, somewhat becoming a part of it. Clerks, workers, policemen, officers, all of them think demanding bribe and kickbacks is their birthright. There are only a few exceptions to this rule, who neither take their part of kickbacks nor even demand it.

Parul: Understandably, the lower strata is corrupt due to public dealings. If we tackle this menace from the top-down manner in the state governments, what results would this yield?

Finance Secretary: In many cases, the upper strata of state governments are found engaging in corrupt practices. People on posts like the commissioner, transport commissioners, district magistrate are also engaged in such practices. Either through cash or by turning a blind eye to the misdeeds being committed. This ensures their posting on plum posts of their desire.

Parul: There has to be a way. Please contemplate on this, take your time.

Finance Secretary: There is not much to this ma'am. See, why does a person resort to such malpractices? Either their work is not being conducted in a desirable manner or they need to get something done above and beyond the law. Most of the people are affected by the first category. In which their government-related work is only accomplished in a timely manner if they partake in giving bribes. The government and/or the department can put out an order that a file should not take more than one, two or three days (or whatever is needed) on one particular seat, to pass to the next. Works that are routine in nature should not take more than one to two days. Any deficit or requirement, if any, should be pointed out to the applicant and resolved immediately and the file be approved to the next person. 50% of corruption or even more will be automatically eradicated. If this is followed properly.

Parul: What about the remaining 50%?

Finance Secretary: The state government is bogged down by various issues. Events like flooding, earthquakes, tsunamis, wildfires need immediate decisions and actions. The corrupt opportunists use these situations to their advantage. The amount of corruption in service items like food packets, medicines, water bottles which are to be distributed to relief camps and lease items such as tents, chairs, blankets, buildings exceeds the corruption in the road and building departments.

Parul: How so?

Finance secretary: When any sort of physical construction like road, buildings, and bridges take place, it is present on paper and physically. It can be audited and inspected. However, items taken on lease such as temporary dwelling like tents for natural disaster victims, food packets, medicines, have no way to be verified physically except for the bills provided. There are no audits to verify the amount purchased for such items. No way to inspect whether the purchase or lease amount shown on bills is the same as ground reality. How many people were provided relief, how many made it to relief camps, how many thousands of medicine and food packets were purchased, the number of chairs, table, lights et al. rented/hired is never truly verified physically? The bills are generated in an arbitrary and fraudulent manner and the pay-out is kept in pockets.

Parul: What is the ultimate solution to all of these?

Finance Secretary: There is only one ultimate solution to this. Our children need to be taught lessons in morality. Hoarding bits of paper (money), soil (pieces of plot and land) and brick and mortar (home/building), etc. is not going to help. There is no happiness in these. True contentment stems from the service of humankind and renunciation. In my opinion, this is the solution, else people have no dearth of options when it comes to theft and fraud. Such vices keep on rising. Despite the fact that the Prime Minister and Chief Minister are honest, there is no drop in bribery and corruption. Only a steady rise. There was this raid conducted at the house of this Member of Parliament. He had amassed so much black money that it took a team of 45 people 18 straight days to account for it all.

I think children should be taught from the level of school about honesty, morality, service, and renunciation and all this should be an integral part of the curriculum. Perhaps then the upcoming generations will be more of an honest and service kind.

Meanwhile, Parul's phone begins to ring. She asks for leave and directs the finance secretary to carve out an action plan. He thanks her and takes his leave.

He has to make preparation for the annual budget. There are decisions to be made about the direction in which to take the budget. The finance secretary and the additional finance secretary arrive to discuss these matters with Parul.

The finance secretary who was a student of history in his time had been selected as an IAS and is now the finance secretary. The additional secretary was a student of economics and is well-read in that subject.

Additional finance secretary RK Raina: The economy of the nation is not favourable at the moment as the inflation rate has reached double digits. The rate of interest has inflated as well. The foreign exchange reserves have been depleted. The value of rupee is falling along with the exchange rate. Usually, a high inflation rate leads to more investment however the demand is dropping therefore investment is being affected. Lesser investment is adversely affecting production, employment, and income. When the currency rate is devalued, the export is supposed to increase however the items which are in demand in the international market, we are unable to supply. The items which can be supplied by us, there are no demands for it in the international market. A condition of stagnation has arrived out of this situation. Important decisions need to be made in this regard to get the nation out of this situation.

Parul: Alright, whatever important steps and decisions are to be taken, you guys go ahead and do it. The budget should be decided in the manner which is favourable for the masses and brings back the economy in line.

Finance secretary D P Tandon: Hard decisions need to be taken and enforced. We need to create demand among the people like JM Keynes did during the recession period of 1929-30. People need to be employed. Employment will lead to a rise in income which in turn will lead to a rise in demand. Naturally, the production increase will follow. This will again increase employment and income, bringing the nation's economy back on the track. However, we need more revenue for all this to happen.

For this, taxation needs to be increased. Although the tax is already high some items that are not taxed already, need to come under its preview. Expansion of items under taxable regions will boost revenue and thus the infrastructure. However, people might not look at its positive side. The opposition will only stress on the part where new items are included in the taxable list, not the positive aspects. Thus collision supporters and even the general public will oppose this move.

Parul: What plan do you guys have in mind? How will the taxes be implemented? What formula will cover all this?

Additional secretary: As the famous finance minister of Louis XIV, Jean Baptiste Colbert said "the art of taxation consists in so plucking the goose as to obtain the largest possible amount of hissing." we will follow the same principle. We need the largest amount of revenue possible with the smallest economic and political damage increased. Now as there is already enough tax burden on the middle class, we need to increase the income tax on the corporate sector.

Parul: The revenue generated in this manner will be spent in which area?

Additional Secretary: In the development of infrastructure, not only will this lead to better roads, more electricity generation, more pure water, better sewage, etc. it will generate more jobs and a reduction in unemployment. This will cause an increase in material and service demands, which in turn will lead to an increase in investment and production. All of this will have a positive impact on the economy of our great Nation. One thing we need to take care of is that we invest in the infrastructure which takes the least amount of time and gestation period. It is because we need an immediate boost to the economy.

Parul: Is there no formula other than Colbert's which can be used? Something even better?

Secretary: Indeed there is Madam. In the Shri Ramcharitmanas, Tulsidas has given another theory. He says that when the sun takes water from the rivers, lakes, wells and the oceans of this earth, nobody realises or takes notice. Water evaporates as per its quantity. However, when the same water is formed into clouds and rains upon the Earth, providing relief from the heat and ample water for farming, everybody takes notice and appreciates it.

We will try our best to follow this theory. We need to bring various areas under the tax umbrella. There are innumerous small shops and establishments such as dhabas, parlours, coaching institutes, cyber cafes, etc. which operate on a smaller level. But do earn a handsome sum of money. They could be taxed which they currently are not. Even if we levy a nominal tax, it could contribute to our overall revenue. And since the tax would be a small nominal amount, it would be insignificant to them while the people will be happy that they are contributing to the Nation's growth. The issue with all of this is that the opposition might make a big issue out of this. Because they will propagate that on the small earner's taxes are being imposed.

Parul: You all should deploy the Tulsidas rule. Nobody will oppose that and the taxes will be levied.

Secretary and additional secretary (together): How come?

Parul: All that needs to be done is that tax is increased on popular items such as petroleum, salt, edibles, etc. You should cover more things under tax and make plans that will boost infrastructure. Only one thing will be the difference-maker.

Secretary: What is that?

Parul: One or two popular consumer items such as petroleum, salt or edibles need to be taxed more.

Additional Secretary: It will not bode well, increasing tax on popular and necessary items.

Parul: See, when the budget is presented, then the opposition will focus on the increased tax rates of the popular items. They will oppose it vehemently. They will not take notice of the newer things which now come under the rules of taxation.

We will then remove those increase tax rates before passing the budget. This will be a win-win situation for all. It will make the opposition and our supporting parties happy. Along with this, the part of the economy which was not monitored will come under the financial regime, thus making the government happy.

Secretary and Additional Secretary praise the talent of Parul Patel. Thus the budget is made and presented in the aforementioned manner. On popular items like petroleum and salt, high taxes are proposed and then taken back. The budget is passed in the Parliament. The rise in inflation is reduced, the demand for items which had reduced, the government creates demand through various methods of investment. There is a boost in the rate of employment and subsidies. The economy seems to be getting back on track.

The Central Bank (RBI) supports the government and makes the necessary changes in Bank rate, MSF, SLR, CRR, repo rate, et al. The economy is boosted and is on the rise.

On the other hand, Parul's place in the party keeps going upwards. Her meteoric rise has insured her place as number 2nd or 3rd after the Prime Minister. Many older Ministers such as the home minister now consider her as their prodigy and wish to see her succeed.

Nonetheless, Parul has now mastered the art of politics. She does not want to play this game of cat and mouse for long. Therefore, according to plan, a video of the second minister in charge goes viral in which he is seen taking bribe for giving a contract for alcohol sale licence.

There has not been even a week since this exposure that there are now allegations of sexual exploitation by a woman. Who knows who is behind all this? The opposition? An old rival or someone at the party? The Minister is flustered by all these events. On the other hand, Parul is successful in convincing the Prime Minister that if a female is made the Deputy Prime Minister, then not only on the national level but this will send a positive message in the international foram too, that the Deputy Prime Minister of the biggest democracy is a woman. This will also positively impact the PM's visage.

So now, Parul has been established as number two in the party in an undisputed manner. She now functionally serves as the Deputy PM of India.

Everything is now happening according to her wishes, expectations, and ambitions. She does not give much thought in taking big decisions. The Prime Minister trusts her like his own. Her hold grows in the political circles. For the welfare of the nations, she takes all the big decisions.

The Prime Minister is scheduled for a foreign visit. Parul is expected to accompany him on the tour. But due to unforeseen reasons, she could not join him. The PM's program goes according to the schedule. He partakes in the conference, where there are many world leaders attending the event. The PM retires for the night in his designated hotel room. He is scheduled to depart for his home country the next morning. God knows how and what happened.

He is found dead in his room the following morning. The news spreads like wildfire and there is a wave of grief gripping the nation. His body is brought back to the nation. The reason for his death is unknown but there are murmurings in media about a cardiac arrest being the reason. The general masses, each, have their own theory. Some cry about a conspiracy, some blame it on rival countries, some blame the opposition, some do agree on the theory being propagated in media. The official report corroborates this. Although the post mortem examination is not conducted.

An emergency meeting is called upon as the PM's cabinet is dissolved. Now a new Prime Minister needs to be elected who will serve for the remainder session. Who knows what to do? The biggest rival of Parul's, in the party, nominates Parul for the post of the PM. Everyone supports this nomination.

Parul takes oath as the Prime Minister and so do the other members of her cabinet. She is now given a freehand to serve the nation.

Every person's life is full of positive as well as negative aspects. When Parul tries to analyse hers, she finds her decisions to be not mature enough. One of them is her decision to get married. On one hand, she had alienated people from her religion by marrying a person from a different religion. And on the other, her marriage has turned out far from ideal. But the silver lining in all this has been that she had kept her maiden name. She decided not to change or convert from her religion at the time of marrying her husband. She had even given her last name/surname to her children.

Some decisions taken by a person have lifelong implications. Perhaps the marriage was her such decision.

On analysing the positive aspects of her life, she finds that not running after monetary gains has been the best decision in her life. She donated and contributed her salary along with the public development funds as much as she could. Be it the Dalits, the exploited sects, the poor, the backward from the society she has done her best to alleviate their situations. Many months ago, as suggested by one forest officer, she brought changes to the forest act so that the tribal living on those land could claim rights to them. She also adds a provision for the conservation of those forests.

Parul's marriage might be far from ideal, but she tries her best to make other's marriage work. She contemplates introducing conjugal visits in jails, as suggested by the jailor. She finds that the only criminal is the person languishing in the gallows. Their spouse has done nothing to deserve physical separation from the person they decided to spend their life with. She also consults the Human Rights Commission regarding this and makes amendments to the Prison Act.

She brings an act, that people who are imprisoned and on whom a sentenced has not been passed, they could be granted conjugal visits on a fortnightly basis whether inside or outside the jail premises. And for those, who are judged as criminals could be given one conjugal visit per month inside the jail premises.

For improving upon scientific research, she introduces Indian Scientific Services on the lines of IAS, IPS, and IFS. The examination for these newly introduced services takes place just after passing the 12th grade, like IITs and medical fields. The persons selected for these services will be provided more necessities than that of the other services. More salary, more allowances, and perks.

The ill practice of reservation has been eradicated from the Scientific and Medical Services. The result of all this is now that all the talented brains who opted for bureaucracy and to serve under politicians were now selected under the ISS and opted for new and revolutionary research. The nation is certainly achieving new feats in this direction. The Nobel Prize for fundamental research is surely looking positive for India.

Only the most intelligent brains are now into the ISS. The field of research and technology has spearheaded new India into the future. Seldom is the case that a Nobel Prize is not won each year. Similarly, be the ordinary masses, the middle class or VIP's everybody's interest is being accounted for.

Cleanliness drive has taken the form of a campaign and now is part of the basic cultural fabric. Where-as before more than 80% of people did not have a toilet at home, now 100% homes not only have a toilet but they are being fully utilised.

Parul has revolutionized the health sector as well. Now the medicines required for a particular disease are mentioned by their molecular names by the doctors and the medical shops too give out medicines on that basis. The unholy communion between the doctors and the big brand pharmacies has now been shattered and the commission system has been eradicated. Therefore the medicinal expenditures have come down around 80% as compared to before.

Parul has got everybody covered under Health Insurance Schemes and so the treatment is covered under insurance and the outdoors medicines are really inexpensive. The children's books now have stories of noblemen and valour of Shivaji, Maharana Pratap, and sacrifice and motivating stories of Mother Teresa. The society now judges the growth and development by thought process, behaviour, service to society and sacrifices done by a person.

Now people who had corruption cases pending on them are not invited as chief guests in various programs. People who contribute the most to our environment and society are now looked upon as a source of pride.

Similarly, everyone is paying their taxes honestly so the issue of electricity, water and roads are now long resolved. Under Parul's regime, the blueprint laid out by the "Raam Rajya" is coming to life.

Parul goes to New York to participate in the annual UN conference. Dorothy's invitation also urges her to return a couple of days after the conference is over. Dorothy's marriage anniversary is the day after the conference and the three musketeers from college will re-unite on the occasion.

Ten

Dorothy's husband George had done a Ph.D. in Economics Science and was teaching at a University. Initially, he was dedicated to teaching but with the passage of time, he is less interested in teaching. It comes to his mind to visualise those economic theories being implemented on the ground level. Gradually, he is influenced by one of the two leading party's principles and becomes an active member of this political party.

George works dedicatedly for the party. The party renders him miscellaneous responsibilities, which he completes efficiently. As time passes on, his contribution to the party increases and becomes memorable. Owing to his capability, ability, capacity understanding, economic acumen, and his activities for the benefit of the party and nation, he is appointed to the post of the member of the council of economic advisor to the President of USA. Later on, seeing his better understanding of national and international level economy, his important role in implementing positive economic change in the country at micro and macro levels and his major contribution in empirical research for the White House along with preparing the best annual economic report for the President, the President deputes him to the post of the chairman of the council of economic advisor.

If your deeds are good, the result is also good. All the religions in the world believe in it and science has also proven it. Some nation gives advice to Dorothy to contest for the post of the general secretary of UNO and she considers it. She decides to contest for the post after seeing and understanding the finesse of the situation. Dorothy has become a veteran of diplomacy and politics in general while working at UNEP. She prepares such an environment to contest for a general secretary that big stalwarts are puzzled before her.

According to the need of the hour, she makes the Asian representatives realize about her being from Asia. She convinces the European leaders and their representatives of her Anglo-Indian origins. To the Americans, she wants to connect by saying that this is her in law's home so her real home. Since she is somewhere in between black and white, she claims to be connected to both of them. Christian, Indian, women, etc. whichever equation suits wherever, she takes advantage of it.

Whatever be the effect of all these equations, but she has become popular because of her good deeds and she is chosen as the general secretary of the UNO. She wins from a huge margin in the global scenario. After she wins and becomes the general secretary of the UNO, it does not bring a difference to her humility or sense of responsibility.

In fact, there are two categories of the people in this world - the one that considers their high post to be a source of more income, respect, happiness and peace and the others who treat it as their responsibility and decide to work harder for it. Dorothy belongs to the second category and fulfills her duty with full dedication and attention.

If it is seen through proper viewpoint, the person who has the greatest responsibility is nobody else but the general secretary of UNO. He/she has to maintain harmony and balance among different countries in the world. He/she has to avoid each and every situation leading to World War - III. He has to see that no smaller or backward country is ignored or left behind in this era of development.

Dorothy is working much harder on her new assignment as the

general secretary of the UNO for world peace and brotherhood. She has become very busy and works for the whole day and even at night. But still, there is one thing that makes her restless, the nuclear weapons. She knows that there are a number of nuclear weapons in the world that can destroy the earth's umpteen times. If a single nuclear weapon falls in the wrong hands, the results could be devastating. What is the need of these nuclear weapons? Why not destroy them from earth?

All this disturbs Dorothy to a great extent. In its initial stages, these nuclear weapons named 'Little Boy' and 'Fat Man' were used on Hiroshima and Nagasaki of Japan in 1945 and the bad effects are still visible after 75 years, so what will be the result of these advanced nuclear weapons if they are used on some country? What will happen if they fall in some wrong hands unknowingly? What will happen if one country uses it in the other country somehow and consequently the other country also uses it? Today nuclear weapons are being tested in scheduled places. For example, Pakistan tested it in Baluchistan province and as a result, the children are born physically or mentally deformed and abnormal in that specific area. So, even to imagine the negative results of the uses of these weapons gives her goosebumps.

Dorothy decides to put all her efforts in ending these nuclear weapons and will agitate the world if it is needed. She thinks that even if she has to run from pillar to post and go for all-out efforts, she will prove the meaningfulness of her life by ending the present nuclear weapons from the globe. She will remain firm and strong until the task is completed. She promises to herself to bring an end to this monster named nuclear weapon.

She will do this auspicious work even if she has to go beyond her work arena. She has a firm belief that if the intentions are good, God also helps. With this strong belief, she puts her wholehearted efforts honestly and dedicatedly to execute this great work. This is a tough task but her intentions are unwavering like Himalaya and

Andes.

Dorothy wishes that all the countries in the world sign on nuclear weapon disarmament and control treaty under the leadership of UNO. It means not only the present weapons will be destroyed but also a treaty that no country will make it in the future.

To implement this noble work, in the first stage she gets prepared a statistical chart of the number and capacity of all the nuclear weapons of America, Russia, France, China, the UK, India, Pakistan, Israel and North Korea, i.e., the countries possessing it. She makes a study of the usefulness or un-usefulness, i.e., profit or loss of nuclear weapons to these countries and also the SWOT-strength, weakness, opportunity, and threat of the specific countries.

She reaches the conclusion that these weapons are useless for these countries. The truth is that the weapons that can destroy God's creation and life, can never be useful for mankind. Most of these countries have kept nuclear weapons because their rival possesses it, as Pakistan has it because its rival country India possesses it. There is no other use of it for Pakistan.

She presents a good formula to destroy all these nuclear weapons from the earth. All the countries will destroy their nuclear weapons themselves in a proper proportion under it.

For instance, if the countries decide to destroy all their nuclear weapons under the guidance and leadership of UNO, the first phase would be disposal of one-third of nuclear weapons like 2183 of USA, 2163 of Russia, 100 of France, 93 of China, 72 of Britain, 50 of Pakistan, 43 of India, 27 of Israel and 7 of North Korea. The second phase would comprise of disposing of another one-third of nuclear cache and finally, the third phase would be disposing of nuclear weapons that are left, therefore going totally nuclear-free when in it comes to weapons.

However, the story won't end here, all the nations of the world will have to decide and promise not to make any new nuclear weapons

A new treaty will be signed superseding PTBT, NPT CTBT et al. wherein all the nations will participate as equals without letting personal gains to hinder it. None of the nations would be allowed to conduct nuclear tests in air, land, water or laboratory. No longer shall nuclear might of a nation be considered the standard-bearer, but the efforts taken by them to establish peace and brotherhood will decide their standing. UNO would publish the annual list of nations who helped the others during the natural calamities like earthquakes, tsunamis floods, epidemic outbreaks.

Dorothy thinks if all of this would be implemented then the human mind will be free of all unwanted fears. Humanity shall be free of the nuclear arms race. No nation would have to bear the cost of manufacturing, installation, and security of nuclear weapons. That cost would now go towards the cause of world peace.

Dorothy holds a meet with representatives of all the nuclear-armed nation however no initial interest is being shown by them on her proposal. Call it a coincidence, that her friend Parul was recently elected as the Prime Minister of India. Dorothy travels officially to India and discusses her proposal with Parul. Parul not only shows her interest in Dorothy's proposal but promises all the help she could give for the cause. It makes Parul Patel, the Prime Minister of India, the first to accept the proposal. Dorothy would then visit Pakistan for her proposal wherein it would promptly be accepted by the Pakistani Prime Minister. This would boost Dorothy's confidence and she decides to meet the president of the United States. She discusses her cause and also stresses how two nations have already agreed to the proposal. She tries and reasons with the President that since the USA and USSR (Russia) have signed treaties like Strategic Arms Limitation Talk (SALT) and Strategic Arms Reduction Treaty (START) to limit the nuclear weapons, it would further their cause of peace, should they decide to accept her proposal. She urges Mr. President that if he ensures such a treaty under his office term, the whole of humanity will be in debt to him.

The President of the United States, after much contemplation, decides to green signal her proposal. He is quite impressed by Dorothy's chain of thoughts and pledges his support to her cause. The American President and the General Secretary of the United Nations would work on their level best and consult others then would meet again after two days to discuss. The agenda on how to implement this worldwide, the logistics are the problem. On this note, they bid goodbyes. Imagine, two of the most powerful leaders decide to act on the same cause, what wonders could they achieve.

The joint effort for the cause of denuclearization of the world bears fruit. The majority of the nations including but not limited to Pakistan, India, Russia, the US, France, Britain agree to it, albeit with some rules and terms. The cause, however, would hit a roadblock in China, Israel, and North Korea.

Now as for as Israel is concerned, it is a democracy and capitalist nation. Some coercion and tactics would let them to green signal the treaty. North Korea has proclaimed that they would only sign on the condition that China signs first. Now, it all boils down to China. How to tackle this situation? How to make them agree?

The president of The United States becomes quite perturbed. He calls a meeting with his counsellors. After much debate and discussion including scientists and specialists from the nuclear field, they come to the decision that if those two Nations will not agree to sign the Treaty, then there should be some sort of restrictions placed on them by the World Trade Organization (WTO) and participating nations. Now, the Chairman of the Council of Economic Advisers, US Mr. George proposes that a proposal called the "Top- 5" shall be implemented.

Mr. President, US: What do you suggest in this proposal?

George: Unlike implementing a complete blanket ban and boycott of the non-participating Nations, the top- 5 proposals would be on the lines of:

a. The top-5 importing partners of the erring Nation would stop import with them.

b. The top-5 export partners will stop export to them.

c. The top-5 providers of raw materials shall cease trade with them.

d. The top-5 FDI, FPI, FII investor's nation, stop investment in that country.

e. The top-5 Tourist Nations issue advisory to the citizen to not visit that country.

f. The top-5 Marine, Land/Road, and Air partner break the relation with that country.

g. The top-5 Defence, Science and Information Technology partner stop co-operation with erring nations.

h. The top-5 Food material, Man-power and Sport partners would decrease the footfall.

i. Every top-5 provider be it political, economic, cultural service et al. would cease to co-operate with the erring Nations.

Mr. President: Could you elaborate on the effects it would have on those Nations?

George: As that Nation will not be able to sell their goods, the demand and supply chain will be affected. With less demand and more supply. They will be forced to cut down the production which would lead to a sharp rise in the unemployment rates. A net reduction in GDP will be taking place. When people will earn less, they will spend less. As a result, demand will reduce after that production, employment, income, and investment et al. would also decline. It will become a vicious cycle. The economy of such a nation would be on the verge of collapsing. Such an event is bound to impact society, politics, law, and order, etc. in that country.

Mr. President: Will the impact be really of such humongous proportions?

George: Absolutely sir, in this era of liberalization, globalization, and privatization, none of the Nations can afford to go against the general sentiments of the world and expect to sustain their trade and economy. The whole world is like a global village. Its actions are interlinked and intertwined. The currency of the erring nation would be devalued. This weakening of the economy and the unavoidable unemployment just might lead to high dissatisfaction among the residents of that nation and there will be an internal conflict.

Mr. President: And?

National Security Advisor, Mr. Ramsey: People will rally and if the nation is not democratic, there will be pressure on it to establish a democracy. If it is already a democracy, the government will begin to rule with an iron hand. The regions and state of the nation would declare Independence. They would then proclaim that they don't need nuclear weapons, they need proper order. They need to connect with the world order so they may take care of their region or state.

Mr. President: What role would we or the UNO play in this?

Mr. Ramsey: A small spark of democracy would bring out democratic leadership to the fore. Its preference would be the greater good of its people, not nuclear weapons. We would facilitate the fruition of such government and leadership. This leadership would boost employment rates, would provide maximum return on investments. This government will boost FDI, FPI, and FII. It will support the poor and needy and will represent the ambitions of the general population.

Mr. President: I see, so in other words this top-5 formula is safe and we can proceed with the idea.

George: Yes sir, Mr. President, the erring nation would be left with only two choices. To go in for denuclearization their weapons, sign our treaty and make a solemn promise not to continue investing in nuclear weapons, therefore saving their Nation from a downward spiral or become a mute spectator in the economical demise of their state. They should sign our treaty within a week and we might not need to take any actions further.

Mr. Ramsey: In other words, the deterrence capability of this top 5 formula is much more than nuclear weapons!

Mr. President: Great!

Mr. President not only agrees to the proposition but is thoroughly convinced and impressed. He has words with the general secretary of the UNO, Dorothy.

These proposals are now introduced in the UN. The participating nations who were opposed to the proposal, soon start to fall in line, fearing reprisal, financial and economic breakdown and end of their ideologies. After much internal debate, they agree to sign the treaty of de-nuclearization, they don't want to be like Czar and Louis's, they don't want the history to repeat itself. Under the aegis of the International Atomic Energy Agency (IAEA), all the nuclear weapons are disposed off in a standardized well-planned manner. The world which had seen and endured the Hiroshima and Nagasaki tragedies was now free from every nuclear tragedy forever.

Today, it is the victory of humanity. The success of the treaty has greatly increased the dignity and prestige of the UNO. The weaker and comparatively backward nations now depend a lot more on the UN. They believe if they can get rid of nuclear weapons, the UN will never let a third world war happen. Dorothy shared the same sentiments and was elated. Not because she is on the most important position, in the world; not because she led the front on the war against nuclear weapons but because she has given her life to the cause of peace and happiness and prosperity of the world. And she has gained quite a success in her mission. On one hand, her efforts have been successful in conservation of the environment, global warming and climate changes have been brought under control and on the other, she has had tremendous success in getting the world rid of nuclear armaments. She had indeed played a vital role in the cause of world peace. And sure takes pride in it.

Humans in their childhood, tend to think about the present and enjoy it. In their youth, they tend to take the future into consideration along with the present and there comes a time when they begin to contemplate the events of the past. Where they have tasted defeat and the important milestones in their life. What was lacking in them? Whom they had high hopes for? Who stepped up and were with them along for the ride, despite no expectations? And who despite high expectations were of no help to them. Dorothy contemplates and analyses and then decides to organise a party to invite all the people close to her and who had played an important role in her life, without any discrimination.

She looks for an opportune movement and day and decides on the last week of the next month. The same day her marriage anniversary takes place and so it will be a perfect occasion to host the party.

After deciding on the date, she dials her closest friends Gurmeet and Parul. She has a long conversation with them and invites the others after.

Dorothy realises that her tenure will be up next year in the UNO and she does not wish to be elected for another term. She wants others to get the opportunity and for the world to get benefits from experiences that will come with others. Therefore she promises her friends that after they all visit her this year in America, she will visit them in India next year.

Days go by slowly and steadily and the day of the anniversary is upon them. All three of them would be assembled at the same place at the same time. Numerous people have arrived from many nations to attend the party. But the mainstay are the three best friends of childhood. Gurmeet and Parul have arrived with their families. Dorothy had urged them to stay for two to three days more and they had obliged. This was logical as they would not get time to talk and spend quality time. Also, the fact that this was Gurmeet's first time in America, so naturally she was to be given the tourist's reception and be shown the great culture and civilization of the United States of America. Parul had only taken two days extra for her visit while Gurmeet was to stay four days after Dorothy's anniversary celebrations.

The auspicious anniversary celebrations take place at Dorothy's home. Contrary to the general expectation, there is no grandeur at the celebrations. Political figures and celebrities are absent from the venue. They were not invited. The two friends seem like chief guest. There are family members of Dorothy and George's parent and their close friends and family. Primarily, the attendees seem like acquaintances of Dorothy and George.

The ceremony is conducted in a simple, decent and placid manner. However, the fun quotient was never low. All the attendees were near and dear ones so there was no fake pomp and show. The ceremony concludes in a planned and peaceful manner. The next day plans were to visit New York City as a tourist.

Everyone visits the main tourist attractions of the great city of New York. They assemble for dinner at night time. After eating dinner, everybody slowly proceeds to their respective rooms to rest for the night. The three friends, Parul, Gurmeet, and Dorothy stay behind.

When friends are exclusive, their success or lack thereof is not discussed. Growth and development are simply not topics of discussion. The main topic is of the days gone by and how they were back in the day. When old, friends meet, friends who are devoid of unnecessary show and trickery; it reminds of the time when Krishna and Sudama met with love, intimacy, calm and affinity. In many ways, the scene at Dorothy's New York situated home could be described as such.

The various life experiences of the trio, which are as much as negative as positive, come to the fore. Like flowers that grow among the thorny bushes, only they know the struggles they have had to go through and suffering they had to put up with. The world does not know the real story behind all their success. And a success it was, in the truest of sense. All three of them had carved a niche for themselves. They had done their bit to discard the thorns from the lives of people and provide peace and prosperity to them, like the flowers.

The night tonight is moonlit, like that other night. A steady wind blows through the night, the atmosphere calm and cool. The scent of flowers permeates the atmosphere. The difference between this night and that night they graduated was the apparent lack of morbid sadness. The lack of fear and panic in the atmosphere. They were successful in getting rid of most of such negativity from the world. The flavour of tonight was happiness, excitement, enthusiasm, and exaltation. No more fear of terrorism, more people serving mankind.

On the topic of terrorism, it is now clear that just like terrorism has no religion, the terrorists have neither. The UNO has passed a resolution now that the dead bodies of slain terrorists will now not be given the funeral in accordance with the religion they claim. Those who bury their bodies will now be burned in waste incinerators while those who burn their dead, will be buried. This will send messages to prospective terrorists that there are no virgins or apsaras after death.

The results are surprising indeed, activities related to terrorism is nowhere to be seen now. After this law has been passed, those prospects now take pride in being friendly towards all other religions as well.

All the nuclear weapons and the fear related to them have been wiped off the face of this Earth. The expenditures wasted in creating and maintaining the nuclear stockpiles are now being utilized for the greater good of the people like development of public amenities and construction of schools, hospitals, rail, road et al. The looming threat of global warming has been contained and the target of warming has been lowered to 1.5 degrees Celsius then the earlier projected 2 degrees.

The religious tussle is very much reduced. The religious stakeholders have now understood that all the combined manpower of the MNC's, after so much of trying could not exterminate something as minute as a mosquito; then how will they succeed in establishing their religious dominance. It is now proven that reaching the apex of societal, political or personal development, is not possible through caste equations, religious appeasement or such trickery but through financial and economic upheaval, combined with proper addressing of societal issues.

It has also been proven that all religions have had orthodox customs and traditions. However, the protection and development of the religion cannot be achieved by holding onto those values but through the integration of modern and scientific methods into it.

The practice of corruption and bribery had permeated the society and now the feeling of charity and social service is being stressed upon. Higher posts in politics or another medium which was considered a seat of power, money, and status are now being seen as a medium and taken of social service. In almost every corner of the world, the basic needs and amenities like food, clothing, shelter, toilet, clean water, and free medical care has been ensured.

In place of dirt, pollution and disease which would dampen the light of spirit, easy and cheap bio-energy are now lighting the homes. Developing countries that would incur huge expenditures on the import of petroleum products have now become an exporter of new and renewable energy and its sources.

Flood, drought and acidic/alkaline soil has now given way to greenery and joy of medicinal plants and flowers whose fragrance permeates all the directions. The mentality of society has undergone a drastic change. Primary men have been the driving force of change and had been at the forefront of development and growth but now women have been at the helm bettering the process and men act as supporters in their mission.

The most important thing is this chain of events is that none of the three friends take credit for any of this. They think of themselves as a medium in achieving the goals they set for themselves back in college. They are happy to be an important link in the great task of growth and development of the world. Orphans who had nobody to support and take care of them were now taking care of the old, the needy and the handicapped.

New conventions have been passed by the UN regarding natural resources such as land, water, and forestry. Most of the countries have now given legal ownership to the aborigines who had been residing in the jungles for millennia. As a result, not only the forests are now safe but are expanding at an ever-increasing rate. People associating with the activities of the Naxalites are now playing an important role in implementing government schemes. With the aforementioned atmosphere of joy and prosperity, looming around the world, the three friends Dorothy Jones, Gurmeet Kaur, and Parul Patel, chat late into the night. It was not personal but was the need of the hour of the world, the circumstances demanded such that when they were in the prime of their youth, they would discuss the world problems and their solution in their college days and now it's the time and age is here finally for it to come to fruition.

Long into the night, they chat and discuss the work they had done, the ups and downs of it all, the laughter and happiness of it, the excitement and various aspects of life and all of it.